OTHER YEARLING BOOKS YOU WILL ENJOY:

YEARLING BOOKS/YOUNG YEARLINGS/YEARLING CLASSICS are designed especially to entertain and enlighten young people. Patricia Reilly Giff, consultant to this series, received the bachelor's degree from Marymount College. She holds the master's degree in history from St. John's University, and a Professional Diploma in Reading from Hofstra University. She was a teacher and reading consultant for many years, and is the author of numerous books for young readers.

For a complete listing of all Yearling titles, write to Dell Readers Service, P.O. Box 1045, South Holland, IL 60473.

Dacia asmus

And Condors Danced

❧✿❀

ZILPHA KEATLEY SNYDER

A Yearling Book

Published by
Dell Publishing
a division of
Bantam Doubleday Dell Publishing Group, Inc.
666 Fifth Avenue
New York, New York 10103

To Larry, as always,
and to my mother, Dessa Jepson Keatley,
whose vivid stories of life
in rural southern California at the turn of
the century were a vital part of my own childhood

ISBN: 0-440-40153-4

Reprinted by arrangement with Delacorte Press

Printed in the United States of America

April 1989

10   9   8   7   6   5   4   3   2

CW

❧❀❧ *chapter 1*

It was midafternoon on an unusually warm June day when Carly Hartwick made the following entry in her secret journal:

> Northeast bedroom, Carlton Ranchhouse, Santa Luisa, Ventura County, California, U.S.A.—Western Hemisphere, World, Universe, Kingdom of God, on the tenth day of June in the year of Our Lord 1907.
>
> **Mehitabel Carlton Hartwick becomes invisible.**

It hadn't been easy—she had been working toward invisibleness for a long time with only partial success—but this time everything had been strangely different.

She had begun, this time, by wishing on a special wishbone. She'd tried wishbones before with no luck at all, but today she used the enormous one that she had been saving ever since Thanksgiving, and it had broken just right. Holding the broken pieces one in each hand, she stood perfectly still for a long time with her eyes closed, willing her skin and bones to disappear, to melt away, to dissolve into nothingness.

The first sign was a strange sensation, a floating feeling of lightness and transparency that grew stronger and stronger, until her feet scarcely seemed to be touching the floor. But she still wasn't satisfied. She began to drift around and around the room, thinking of will-o'-the-wisps and gossamer and other light and airy things, all the while humming a high-pitched tune that got softer and softer until it died away to nothingness. By the time the last feathery whisper ended, she was absolutely certain. Moving slowly and softly so as not to break the spell, she pulled her journal out from under the mattress and recorded the miraculous event. Then she went out to make the final test.

The upstairs hallway of the old ranch house was dark and stuffy, a long tunnel smelling of heat and dust. Outside the door of her room the invisible Mehitabel Carlton Hartwick, commonly known as Carly, paused for only a moment before gliding through the dim light to the head of the narrow staircase, and on down to the back hall. Turning into the dining room, she crossed it silently and confidently—absolutely certain that she wouldn't be noticed. And wouldn't have been—even if someone had been in the room. So far so good, but next came the most difficult test—the parlor. There were people in the parlor, two very important people, Anna and Lila Hartwick, Carly's mother and sister.

Anna Hartwick was lying on the sofa reading a book and Lila was standing near the window when Carly walked right between them and out the front door. She walked slowly and deliberately, and it was perfectly obvious that neither her mother nor her sister had any idea that she was anywhere within a hundred miles.

On the broad veranda Carly leaned against the wall and shivered with excitement. She had decided on becoming invisible on her tenth birthday just over a year ago, and since then she had tried everything without success. During that time she had used all kinds of charms and rituals and even prayers, but nothing had worked.

There had been times, of course, when she felt it had almost happened; when it really seemed that not one member of her family had seen or heard her for hours at a time. Always before it had turned out to be only her imagination; but today was different. Carly's shoulders lifted and then fell slowly in another long-drawn-out, delicious shiver.

A familiar combination of sounds—the clop of hooves and jingle of harness—seeped through her invisible shield, and she turned toward the road. A team and wagon was coming down from the high valley. She moved out to the veranda railing for a better view. It was the Díazes' buckboard, and old Mr. Díaz was driving the team. Welcoming another test, perhaps not a terribly difficult one, since Grandpa Díaz was known to be nearsighted, she stayed right where she was, and even raised a hand in a daring wave.

The wagon clopped and jingled by, trailing a cloud of dust, and Grandpa Díaz gave no sign that he had noticed that someone, in plain view on the veranda steps, was waving to him. She was definitely invisible.

Concentrating again, willing invisibleness with her total being, she began the return trip and the final trial. Silently, she opened the screen door and glided back into the parlor. On the red velvet fainting couch her mother continued to read, and at the window Lila went on staring up the dusty valley road. Across the room, and out the door, and down the hall, she went, a silent, unseen presence.

A moment later she swept triumphantly into the kitchen—

and a voice said, "Carly dear, you're just in time to lend me a finger."

Nellie, Carly's oldest sister, was at the kitchen table wrapping a parcel. She pulled the string tighter and nodded toward the spot where a pressing finger would insure a tight knot. "They're molasses cookies for Aunt Mehitabel. Arthur's going to run them over for me, and you know Arthur. If they're not carefully wrapped he'll have half of them eaten and the rest smashed before he gets out of the yard."

Carly stood motionless, staring at her sister in dismay. Wouldn't you just know it would be Nellie who would spoil it all? A person just couldn't be invisible, or anything else wondrous and extraordinary around someone like Nellie— someone who insisted on seeing everything in such an ordinary way.

"Carly?" Nellie asked, still waiting with the string pulled tight. Mehitabel Carlton Hartwick, the ex-invisible person, clumped dejectedly to the table and put her finger on the knot. As Nellie's head bent over the package, Carly rolled her eyes upward and made faces at the ceiling—tragic despair —bitter grief—and then, as she looked down at her sister's carrotty red head, a kind of puzzled wonder. It was amazing, unbelievable actually, that three sisters could be so different. Magical, mysterious, almost invisible Mehitabel; and Lila— Lila the Fair, Lila the Lovable, Lila the Lily-Maid of Santa Luisa—and then there was Nellie.

"What is it, Carly?" Nellie finished with the string and looked up, pushing a straggle of curly red hair off her freckled forehead. "What's the matter?"

"Oh, nothing. Nothing at all. Why did you think something was the matter?"

Nellie smiled. "Oh, I don't know. Would you like a cookie? I saved some especially for you. They're in the pantry."

Carly was in the pantry eating a cookie and putting several others in her pinafore pocket when she heard a stomping of boots and a jingle of spurs. Spurs! Stuffing the rest of the cookie into her mouth, she shot out into the kitchen, and nearly collided with her brother. "Arthur," she said through a mouthful of crumbs, "are you riding Comet to Aunt Mehitabel's? I thought you were walking. If you're riding Comet, may I come too?"

Arthur and Nellie laughed. "Would you mind spraying that again?" Arthur said, brushing cookie crumbs off the front of his leather vest.

Carly gulped and swallowed and said, "Could I ride to Aunt Mehitabel's with you? I really ought to go see her, Nellie. I haven't been since Tuesday. I promised her I'd come today." It was the truth. She'd almost forgotten, but she had promised.

"You'll have to walk home," Arthur said. "I'm going on into town after I leave off the cookies."

"I don't mind," Carly said. "May I go? May I, Nellie?"

"You'll have to ask Mama."

"Oh, why? She'll just say to ask you. When Father isn't here she always says to ask you."

Nellie shook her head, frowning, as if she resented being reminded that she was in charge. It was a response that had always puzzled Carly. She herself would not have minded being in control of almost anything, she was sure of that. But Nellie had always been the one to ask when Father was away, even though Arthur and Lila were just a little younger, and Charles was even older than Nellie herself. But then Charles, Carly's oldest brother, who was twenty-one and a grown man in some ways, just wasn't much good at being in charge.

"Well?" Arthur asked, grinning at Nellie. "Am I to be saddled with the infant as far as Auntie's, or not?"

Carly couldn't help giggling. Arthur, at eighteen, was so

13

much bigger than twenty-year-old Nellie; and his face, lean and dark and already shadowed by the beginnings of a beard, looked much older than his sister's. Arthur got the joke. Looking down at Carly, he returned her grin and then, turning again to Nellie, he said in a high-pitched little boy's voice, "May we go, Mummy? Will you let us go to Auntie's?"

Nellie smiled reluctantly. "Well, let's tell Mama you're going, at least. She may want you to take a message to Aunt M. Come on, now." She turned to her brother. "Wait a minute, Arthur. This won't take long."

In the dimly lit parlor neither Anna nor Lila seemed to have moved an inch. "Mama," Nellie said. "Mama!" And Anna Hartwick put her finger on the page to hold her place and slowly raised her dark head—dark like Lila's and almost as beautiful, in spite of the gray strands in her hair and the dark hollows around her eyes.

"Listen," she said. "Isn't this lovely? Come here, girls. Let me read this to you." She raised the book to show the title. "It's from *The Old Curiosity Shop*."

Before she even began to read, Carly knew it would be about Petey. Once in a while Mama read about other things, verses about autumn colors or snow or yearning for your native land. But more often, as now, what she read was related in some way to Petey.

" 'When Death strikes down the innocent and young, for every fragile form from which he lets the panting spirit free, a hundred virtues rise, in shapes of mercy, charity, and love, to walk the world, and bless it.' " There was a quaver in Mama's voice as she read, and when she raised her eyes Carly could see the gleam of tears. The innocent and young. Poor little Petey. She felt her own eyes began to fill, but remembering Arthur and Comet, she blinked hard and nudged Nellie to remind her of the business at hand.

"It's beautiful, Mama," Nellie said. "It really is. But just now we need to know if it's all right if Carly goes to Aunt M.'s with Arthur. I'm sending her some cookies."

"To Aunt M.'s?" Mama sighed and shrugged. "Yes, I suppose so. Now that school is out, I suppose Aunt Mehitabel will be expecting to have her little pet right there at Greenwood most of the time." Mama sighed again and smiled sadly at Carly. "But isn't it awfully warm to walk such a long way? Arthur will take the surrey, won't he?"

"Father has the surrey," Carly reminded her, "but Arthur's taking me on Comet. At least on the way down and . . ."

Mama's eyes had gone back to her book. "Yes," she said. "Yes, that should be all right. Give Aunt Mehitabel my love."

"All right, Carly." Nellie turned to go and Carly followed, glancing back over her shoulder.

Mama was reading again and Lila had gone back to the window. Against the light Lila made a slender silhouette, the high collar of her white shirtwaist emphasizing her long, graceful neck. Masses of dark hair wreathed her small head and then fell down her back in a heavy braid. Her face was turned away, but Carly knew her beautiful dark eyes would be clouded and distant. "Daydreaming again," people said about Lila when her eyes were like that, but Carly knew it was more than that. Lila was in love. Sixteen-year-old Lila Hartwick was in love with Johnny Díaz and had been for almost as long as Carly could remember. No one else knew. It was a tragic secret love and terribly sad and exciting and Carly would never never tell anyone.

Halfway out the door she turned and ran back. Putting her hand on Lila's arm, she waited until the dreamy eyes turned away from the window. "Good-bye, Lila," Carly said, trying to make her voice ordinary and matter-of-fact while her eyes spoke volumes. "I'm going to Aunt M.'s, with Arthur. Do you want us to say hello to anyone for you? I mean anyone we might meet on the road?"

Lila's smile was vague and lovely. "No," she said. "No. I don't think so."

❀❀❀ *chapter 2*

Arthur and Comet were waiting impatiently in the shade of the walnut tree in the backyard. Arthur was frowning and slapping his quirt against his booted leg, and Comet was tossing his head and pawing the ground. At the sight of them Carly instantly forgot the dimly lit parlor and Dickens and poor little Petey and even lovely Lila's sad secret.

"It's all right," she said, bouncing with excitement. "I can go." She grabbed for the saddle horn and was jumping on one foot, trying to reach the stirrup with the other, when Tiger appeared out of nowhere and almost knocked the other leg out from under her.

Tiger was Carly's dog and dearest friend, next of course to her family and Aunt M. and Woo Ying. He was small and white with brown spots and funny brown eyebrows, with a hint of Scotch terrier in his appearance and feisty disposition. Next to Carly and food, he loved going places, and at the moment he was obviously planning to go wherever Arthur and Carly were going.

"Uh-oh," Carly said, recovering her balance. "We can't let

him follow. I promised Aunt M. I wouldn't bring him next time I came. Woo Ying is mad at him for digging up his petunias. I'll tie him up."

"I'll do it," Arthur said. "It'll take you forever. Here! Hold the reins." He grabbed Tiger's collar and pulled him toward the doghouse. For a moment Carly watched, sharing Tiger's bitter disappointment as he skidded over the ground, his feet braced in a hopeless attempt to avoid the hated tether. But then she turned her attention to the high-strung colt and forgot about poor Tiger.

Holding the reins tightly, she crooned a soothing hymn of praise and admiration, while the powerful dark bay colt sidled around her and rolled his bit, testing the authority of the hands that held him. Completely focused on her exciting task, she was only vaguely aware of Tiger's whimpers as he was tied to the doghouse, and of Nellie and Arthur's conversation. But, a minute later, as she was being boosted up onto Comet's back, she began to hear what Nellie was saying.

"Just don't let her ride astride again with her skirt hiked up halfway to her waist," Nellie said. "You remember what Father said last time."

"But, Nellie," Carly said, "it's a lot safer that way. It's so hard to keep your balance riding sidesaddle."

"I know. But you're a big girl now and if you're going to ride horses you must learn to ride like a lady. And you'll be safe enough if Arthur keeps Comet down to a walk."

Carly knew there was no point in saying that that wasn't the kind of ride she had in mind. So she kept quiet and sat sideways on the saddle skirt, hanging on to Arthur's belt with both hands. It was true that Father had ruled that Carly was too old to ride astride in public places, but Carly knew from experience that Arthur never took rules too seriously, not even Father's. And, sure enough, once out on the valley road she was able to talk her brother into not only allowing her to

18

sit astride, but also into letting the fretting, sidestepping Comet stretch his legs in a quick gallop.

It was wonderful; the wind in her face, her hair flying, the smell of the dusty road and the sweating horse, and the smooth rhythmical surge as the ground flew beneath them. Down the long, flat stretch of road between tall rows of Carlton walnut trees, and then up the slow rise to the foothills of the Mupu Ridge, they raced in only a few wonderful minutes. But suddenly it ended. As they topped the slope, Arthur pulled Comet to a quick stop. "Buggy coming," he said. "Be quick now. As you were, Infant."

Going from sidesaddle to astride and back again was a risky operation, but one at which Carly was well practiced. It involved a quick push backward and then a daring leg over while balanced near the horse's tail. By the time the Hamiltons' sorrel mare trotted past with Mrs. Hamilton peering out and waving, Carly was seated properly with her skirt and pinafore down below her knees.

In front of Greenwood, Aunt Mehitabel's big house on the edge of town, Arthur pulled Comet to a stop, reached back for Carly's hand, and swung her to the ground. The horse was fretting again, wanting to run, and the moment Arthur loosened the reins he leapt forward—and Carly remembered and yelled, "The cookies!"

Arthur pulled up so sharply that Comet reared. His black mane flying, his hooves pawed the air before he came down to dance sideways across the road. Controlling the prancing horse with one hand, Arthur pulled the package of cookies from the saddlebag and tossed them to Carly with a grin. A moment later horse and rider were off toward town in a cloud of dust. Clutching the cookies in both arms, Carly watched and let her mind race with the racing horse.

Arthur of the Pony Express—Arthur the handsome young Pony Express rider on his powerful dark steed pursued by a war party of Indians—Indians everywhere—but they'll never catch him—not on his wonderful horse—the fastest horse in the whole world.

It wasn't until the dust cloud had entirely faded away that the dream faded too. Carly sighed deeply, gathered up imaginary reins, and galloped toward Greenwood.

Carly Hartwick, Pony Express rider, galloped through dangerous Indian territory on her beautiful black stallion, her right hand holding the reins while her left clutched the mail pouch against her chest. The mail pouch smelled like molasses cookies.

The smell reminded her of the cookies in her pocket. Pulling her spirited steed to a rearing, prancing stop, she glanced quickly around her. No Indians in sight. She dismounted and tied the reins to a nearby sagebrush—actually one of Woo Ying's flowering plums, but in Indian territory it would most likely be sagebrush.

Fishing in her pocket, the Pony Express rider found that her food ration for the long dangerous ride had been reduced to crumbs. No doubt struck by the arrow that had grazed her leg. A bad wound, but not fatal. She'd made it. The ride was over and the mail had gone through. Her mission had been accomplished.

She limped, favoring the wounded leg, to the garden bench next to the petunia bed, sat down, and gave her full attention to the contents of her pocket. Nothing but crumbs, all right. She must have bounced on them while Comet was galloping. She sighed. After a moment she pulled her pinafore pocket up to her mouth and stuck her tongue in among the cookie crumbs. Suddenly she was the black stallion, enjoying his nosebag of oats at the Pony Express rest stop. She nickered contentedly and munched molasses-flavored oats.

"You sick, Miss Carly?"

Carly sat up with a start and pulled down her pinafore. It

was only Woo Ying. "You shouldn't sneak up on people like that," she said sternly. "You scared me."

"Missy sick?" Woo Ying asked again. "Why apron over face?"

Carly giggled. "I'm fine," she said, brushing cookie crumbs off her chin. "Look. I brought Auntie some cookies."

Woo Ying took the package and shook it gently. "You make?" he asked, and suddenly his wrinkled face became a mask of terror. "You try poison Woo Ying again?"

Carly laughed. She laughed so hard she choked on cookie crumbs. Woo Ying was always teasing and lately his favorite tease was about the cake she'd baked for him and Aunt M. a few weeks ago. Woo Ying had been down with the lumbago and Aunt M. had been trying to cook, and making a mess of it as usual, so Carly had offered to make a lemon cake. Lemon cake was one of Nellie's specialties and Carly had watched her make it many times. Hers would have been just as good as Nellie's, too, if Aunt M. hadn't been trying to reorganize Woo Ying's kitchen.

"I didn't try to poison you, Woo Ying," Carly was finally able to gasp. "You know I didn't. It was Aunt M. who put the salt in the sugar bin. It wasn't my fault."

"Don't know." Woo Ying shook his head slowly, his face a caricature of suspicion. "Think you try poison poor Woo Ying." Suddenly he stopped playing. "Come on in house now, missy. See poor Auntie."

❧❀❧ *chapter 3*

As the old man in his soft black slippers shuffled down the brick path through the beautifully tended garden, Carly skipped beside him.

"Poor Auntie?" she asked. "Is Aunt M. sick?"

"No. No sick. Lonely. Aunt M. miss you. Why missy not come Greenwood? School all done. Got lots of time. When missy not come Aunt M. very sad. When Aunt M. sad—very cross. Yell at poor Woo Ying all time."

Carly giggled. "And you yell right back," she said. "I'm sorry. Really I am. It's just been so hot. It's a long way to walk when it's so hot. But I'm here now, so don't be cross."

Woo Ying glared angrily at her and she giggled again. That terribly fierce scowl had been a joke between them ever since she could remember. Nothing went back farther in her memory than the games she played with Woo Ying. She could even remember when she'd been so small that he put her on a chair beside him while he made dinner, so she could play at cooking. That must have been before her fifth birthday when she was still living at Greenwood.

22

She knew her fifth birthday had been after she'd gone to live with the rest of the Hartwicks. She would always remember how she had cried on that day because Woo Ying wasn't there for her cake and presents. She'd always remembered how sad she'd been on that birthday. But the next day had been wonderful. Aunt M. and Woo Ying had come to bring another present. And the present had been the best one Carly had ever received—a fat white puppy with funny brown eyebrows who was fiercely Tigerish even then, when he still walked with a puppy wobble.

Aunt M. was not in the parlor, dining room, or in the library. In the library Carly stopped for a moment to inspect a recently opened book packet on the desk near the windows. Just as she suspected, it was from Sears, Roebuck, and it contained several new Bertha Clay romances. Carly and Aunt M. loved Bertha Clay romances. Aunt M. said that romances were their secret vice, hers and Carly's—a secret that was not to be shared with such persnickety people as the members of the Santa Luisa Ladies' Literary Society or, of course, Carly's father.

"Trash, I know," Aunt M. said, about Mrs. Clay's exciting stories. "But harmless enough, and it's my opinion that one needs a little relief from edification now and again."

Carly agreed. At least she loved Mrs. Clay's beautiful romantic heroines and dashing heroes and all their terrible tragic problems followed by comfortably reliable happy endings. She hoped Aunt M. would hurry and read this bunch so she could borrow them. The top book in the packet, *Love's Chain Broken,* looked fascinating, and Carly was skimming the first page when Woo Ying called her.

"You come, missy? Woo Ying find Auntie M."

Mehitabel Carlton, Carly's great-aunt, was working in the greenhouse. Wearing a loose gardening smock over her green dimity, she was watering ferns with a long-necked watering can. Her back was toward them, but when she heard the squeak of the greenhouse door she began to shout without even bothering to turn around. "Where have you been, you lazy Chinaman? I've been calling and calling."

"No hear you call," Woo Ying shouted back. "Tell Woo Ying work in garden, Woo Ying work in garden. More better stop yelling, old woman. Got company."

"Company?" Aunt Mehitabel turned quickly. "Carly, you good-for-nothing child. Where have you been?" She held out her arms and Carly ran into them and was enfolded in a violent hug and the combined odors of lavender and household ammonia.

They finished the watering together, with Aunt M. wielding the watering can while Carly and Woo Ying followed along behind—talking. Carly talked and Woo Ying talked and sometimes they both talked at once. Carly told about the picnic on the last day of school and the new batch of ducklings and other news from the ranch house, while Woo Ying pointed out plants that had been forgotten and scolded about others that had been given too much or too little water. Finally Aunt M. shoved the can into his hands. "All right!" she said. "Do it yourself, you tiresome old wretch. Carly and I are going into the parlor. When you've finished, you can come in and make us some tea."

As Aunt M. led her out of the greenhouse, Carly looked back over her shoulder and grinned at Woo Ying. "In the kitchen," she said to Aunt M. "Let's have tea in the kitchen." Having tea in the kitchen was always a lot more fun because Woo Ying would sit down and join them. In any other room of the house he insisted on behaving like a proper servant, standing at attention near the door while they ate and drank.

Woo Ying liked everything to be proper, and he'd always had very definite ideas about what was proper and what wasn't. But standing at the door like a proper servant had never kept him from shouting and yelling. And since he couldn't hear too well from across the room, the things he shouted didn't always make much sense.

"Why say Woo Ying telling lies," he'd yelled once when Aunt M. was telling about the wonderful fly trap he'd invented. "Woo Ying not ever telling lies."

"Killing flies, you crazy Chinaman," Aunt M. had yelled back. "I said you've been killing flies."

Carly had to run to Woo Ying to explain, and then they had all laughed. Carly always laughed at the shouting and yelling at Aunt M.'s, even though some people thought it was disgraceful and embarrassing. Carly had tried once to explain it to her mother; to make Mama understand how there were different kinds of shouting and how the kind that Aunt M. and Woo Ying did wasn't at all embarrassing. "Do you mean because they don't really mean it?" Carly's mother had asked. "Oh, they mean it." Carly grinned. "They mean it, all right. It just isn't—serious." Mama had shaken her head with sad disapproval, and Carly said stubbornly, "Well, I like it, anyway."

But even more entertaining than the shouting was the conversation when the three of them sat around the kitchen table. Sometimes when they were sitting together Carly could get the two of them to tell about the olden days. There was nothing that she liked better than hearing Aunt M. and Woo Ying talk about the olden days in Santa Luisa, and the even more olden days when Aunt M. was growing up in Maine and Woo Ying in China.

❧❀❧ *chapter 4*

Some of Carly's favorite stories were the ones Woo Ying told about his childhood in China and how he had gotten to California as a stowaway during the gold rush when he was only a boy. He'd had a terrible time on the ship and had almost starved to death before the sailors found him. After that he had to work very hard in the ship's galley and was sometimes beaten, but at least he had enough to eat. He'd been told that he would be sent back to China when they reached San Francisco, so as soon as the ship docked he jumped overboard and swam to shore. He'd wanted to be a gold miner but after he made his way to the goldfields, he found that Chinese gold miners were not much safer than Chinese stowaways. In fact he was about to be shot by some evil miners when he was rescued by a kind and brave prospector named Edward Carlton. The same Edward Carlton, of course, who later became Aunt M.'s husband.

All of Woo Ying's olden-days stories were full of terribly exciting things like narrow escapes and beatings and starvation and evil people with knives and guns. Aunt M.'s stories were interesting in different ways.

Aunt M. had grown up in a small town in the state of Maine, and although her early days hadn't been nearly as dangerous as Woo Ying's, she had fascinating stories to tell about such strange things as storms called blizzards that buried everything under huge drifts of snow.

But the part of Aunt M.'s life that Carly liked best was the love-story part. Aunt M., who was Mehitabel Johnson then, was only fourteen years old when she fell in love with a neighbor named Edward Carlton. According to Aunt M., she had mooned around for weeks before she discovered that the tall, handsome neighbor had proposed to Miranda, her older sister. Edward and Miranda became engaged, but in the meantime the California Gold Rush started, and in 1850 Edward Carlton joined the rush to the goldfields. He promised to come back for Miranda as soon as he made his fortune, but it had taken much longer than anyone expected, and Miranda had grown tired of waiting. Two years after Edward Carlton went away, a new young minister named Everett Hartwick came to the Presbyterian church that the Johnsons attended, and he and Miranda fell in love and were married.

Years passed and Aunt M. finished school and became a teacher. Edward Carlton had written to her now and then while he was engaged to her sister, and afterward their correspondence had continued. When he wrote that he had finally made a small strike, she'd hoped that he might soon return to Maine, but that was not to be. Instead he had decided to buy land and settle in southern California. But their correspondence continued, a friendly but rather formal exchange of letters between old friends, until 1869 when a very special letter was delivered to Mehitabel Johnson. It was from Edward Carlton and he wanted to know if she would consider coming to California to be his wife.

27

Carly was particularly interested in that part of the story. Sometimes, alone in her bedroom, she would act it out. She would be the young Mehitabel Johnson, sitting at her window, crying and staring out at mountainous snowdrifts. In Carly's imaginings there were always blizzards in Maine. Having never seen snow except from afar on the tops of distant mountains, she yearned for blizzards and snowdrifts, and included them whenever possible. So there was always snow in Aunt M.'s story—snow and tears.

The crying was necessary, of course, because her heart was still broken. Carly had always been good at producing tears more or less at will, a talent envied by a few of her friends, but regarded with suspicion by others. So she would sit at the window crying real tears and staring out into a shimmering white landscape, until a postman appeared holding a letter over his head as he struggled through shoulder-high waves of rapidly drifting snow.

Sometimes she went on to act out the rest of the story—the bidding farewell forever to Maine and all her old friends and the long, dangerous, and uncomfortable trip to California in the very early days of the transcontinental railway. And then there was the meeting with Edward Carlton, her true love, after almost twenty years of separation.

But today, even though Aunt M. agreed to having tea in the kitchen, she didn't seem to be in the mood for stories about the past. "Where has your father been?" she demanded while she was still filling the teapot at the kitchen sink pump. "I haven't seen him in three days."

Carly was feeding the fire in the huge gleaming stove. The stove, a magnificent Princess, the most regal of kitchen ranges, had six burners and two enormous ovens. Woo Ying's pride and joy, it was always polished and blacked to perfection. In the wintertime it was the center of the house, a warmth-giving, comforting presence, but now in the summer heat it was less inviting. Gingerly, Carly scraped the remaining coals into a pile and added a few small sticks.

"Father went to Ventura," she said, "to see about getting some extra hands for the apricot pitting. Charles went with him. They're supposed to be back tomorrow."

"Oh, yes, I'd forgotten that he was planning to go this week." Aunt M. pulled out a chair and sat down at the round oak table. Her voice had a tense, edgy sound as she went on. "He might have stopped by before he left. I've something important to discuss with him. And now he won't be back until tomorrow." She brushed imaginary crumbs off the table with quick, irritable sweeps of her hand. "Should have been able to telephone him," she muttered. "Lines could have been up the valley months ago, and they would have been, too, if certain people hadn't been pulling strings."

Carly sat down next to her. Leaning on her elbows with her chin in her hands, she looked carefully at the wrinkle-furrowed face of her great-aunt before she said, "What's the matter? What's happened, Aunt M.?"

"Nothing's happened. That is, nothing's happened yet. But I've had another letter from Quigley. He's after the spring water again. And he says that this time he's going to get it."

"Aiii!" The angry shriek from directly behind her made Carly jump even though she recognized it immediately as the sound Woo Ying always made when things didn't go to suit him. "Aiii!" he always shouted when the toast burned or the biscuits didn't rise, or when anyone so much as mentioned Alfred Bennington Quigley.

Many years ago Alfred Quigley had been Edward Carlton's partner. By the time Edward died in 1894, Quigley was the biggest landowner in the Santa Luisa Valley and he had decided that all of the Carlton land should be his too. He had tried to buy the Carlton holdings from Aunt M., but she had refused his offer. Instead she asked her nephew, Ezra Hartwick, to come to California to take over as foreman of the ranch. Ezra agreed, and that was why Carly's family had come all the way from Maine to California. But even after the Hartwicks had arrived and Carly's father had taken over as manager of the ranch, Quigley had not given up.

Woo Ying said Quigley would never give up. "Aiiii! Devil Quigley never give up." Carly had heard him yell it enough times to be used to it. But this time Woo Ying had come into the kitchen so quietly in his soft black slippers that she hadn't known he was there, and his sudden shout had made her jump.

"Stop that," Aunt M. said. "I've told you and told you not to make that dreadful noise. It's enough to scare a body out of their wits."

Woo Ying shrugged, muttered something in Chinese, and shuffled into the pantry. A moment later he came out carrying a loaf of bread and a huge knife. All the time he was slicing and buttering the bread he went on muttering to himself and occasionally swishing the knife around his head as if he were charging into an army of attacking Quigleys. Carly poked Aunt M. and nodded at Woo Ying.

"Look at Woo Ying," she whispered, grinning.

"I know," Aunt M. said, frowning sternly. "Crazy old coot." Carly giggled and she said it again. "Crazy old coot." But this time she was smiling.

❧✿❧ *chapter 5*

The sun was low and long shadows were creeping over the Santa Luisa Valley by the time Carly left Greenwood and started the long walk home. At the gate she turned to wave good-bye. Aunt M. and Woo Ying had come out on the veranda to see her off. Clanging the wrought-iron gate shut behind her, she waved once more and started down the dusty road, swinging a carefully wrapped package by its neat string handle. In the package were some books she was borrowing from Aunt M.'s library, some horehound drops, and a few Chinese nuts.

The horehound drops and the nuts were supposed to be a surprise, but she'd seen Woo Ying slip them into the package. Actually she didn't care much for horehound, but Lila liked it. Carly always saved her horehound for Lila.

The books were *King Arthur and His Knights of the Round Table* and *Rebecca of Sunnybrook Farm,* both of which she had read before, and two new ones. One of the new ones was *Love's Chain Broken,* which she'd managed to talk Aunt M. out of even though she'd not yet read it herself, and another called *The Adventures of Sherlock Holmes.* She couldn't wait to read that one because Aunt M. had hinted that Father might find Sherlock Holmes even more unsuitable than Bertha Clay.

"Is it too stimulating?" Carly had asked hopefully. "Too stimulating" was what Father said about most of her favorite books.

"Probably," Aunt M. had said shortly, and then walked out of the room muttering something about stimulating being better than suffocating.

A little way beyond Greenwood the road forked where the Hamilton Valley Road sloped northward from Santa Luisa Avenue. Taking the north fork, Carly soon came in sight of the tops of the tall shade trees and the third-story tower of the Quigleys' house. In the *Santa Luisa Ledger* there were often announcements such as "The Women's Relief Corps met Wednesday last, at Citronia, the handsome estate of the Quigley-Babcock family." The Babcocks were old Alfred Quigley's daughter, Alicia, her husband, Elmer Babcock— and Henry. Henry Babcock was Alfred Quigley's only grandchild—and the biggest pest and bully in the Santa Luisa Grammar School.

Carly stopped when she was opposite the entrance with its huge stone pillars and the sign that arched above them spelling out the ridiculous name in elaborately ornamented letters —CITRONIA! But Aunt M. never called it that. "Ridiculous name," she always said whenever it was mentioned. Curling her lip sarcastically, she would drawl "Ci-tron-i-a," making it sound ri-di-cu-lous, and Woo Ying would throw up his hands and go "Aiii!"

"Citronia," Carly whispered, peering down the curving graveled driveway to where she could catch a glimpse of the scrolls and curves and loops and bulges of the veranda's fancy woodwork. "Ci-tron-i-a! Aiii!"

Dropping her package onto a patch of dry grass, she began to slice the air with both hands. "Aiii!" she yelled, jumping from side to side and slashing and jabbing. "Aiii!"

Just then a wagon turned onto Hamilton Road from Arnold Street and Carly froze in mid-slash. Picking up her package, she continued on her way in such a ladylike manner that she was soon overtaken by the wagon, which turned out to be Dan Kelly's buckboard.

The Kellys were the Hartwicks' nearest neighbors. Their homestead was in the foothills above the Carlton land in an area that had always been called Grizzly Flats. Dan Kelly was what people called a real old-timer. He'd lived in the Santa Luisa Valley since the early days and knew the area better than anyone, particularly the wilderness way back in the Sespe Mountains. He could tell wonderful stories about such things as grizzly bears and cougars, and ordinarily Carly would have been glad for a visit with him. But not when he'd just seen her pretending to be a Chinese hatchetman.

"Bless me, if it's not little Carly Hartwick," Dan said as he pulled alongside. His eyes were crinkling in the way they always did when he was teasing. "And here I was wondering what grand young lady was traipsin' up our way at this hour of the evening."

"Hello, Mr. Kelly," Carly said, tucking her head and looking up at him sideways to hide a hot flush of embarrassment. Even though he was pretending he hadn't, she was sure he'd seen what she was doing back there in front of the Quigleys'.

Leaning down from the buckboard's seat, Mr. Kelly extended his hand. "Hop up here beside me, lass, and keep me and my old mules company as far as the Carlton place. 'Tis a long, dusty way for such a grand young lady to be going by shank's mare."

Carly shook her head. "Thank you, Mr. Kelly, but I think

I'll walk. I'm used to it. I walk to my aunt's place quite often."

"Well, now, I know you do, and the cool of the evening, 'tis a grand time for walkin'. Perhaps you'll be visiting us at the Flats soon?"

"Oh, yes," Carly said. "I'll try to. Tell Matt to come for me —on the donkeys."

"I'll do that very thing," Dan said. "We'll be looking forward to seeing you. Maggie and meself, and Matt most of all." Dan Kelly slapped the reins across the mules' backs, waved his hand, and the buckboard pulled slowly away, creaking and groaning.

With the wagon out of sight around the first curve, Carly abandoned her ladylike pace in favor of her usual gait, a skipping, running walk that at times broke into a gallop—and in only a few minutes she passed the outskirts of Santa Luisa —and soon afterward the last telephone pole.

Carly had been waiting for the arrival of telephone lines in the Hamilton Valley with great impatience. It would be wonderful to be able to crank the handle and chat with friends who were miles away. But what she was looking forward to even more was being able to pick up the phone when other people's numbers rang, and listen in on their conversations. That, she thought, would be a lot like becoming invisible— and important for the same reasons. But the poles had not yet gone up the valley, and that, according to Aunt M., was because of "string pulling." And the string puller was, of course, Alfred Quigley.

Carly looked around her where, at that very moment, she was surrounded by Quigley lemon orchards. On both sides the dome-shaped trees, their crisp, shiny leaves glittering in the slanting sunlight, crowded the Hamilton Valley Road into a narrow, dusty alley. Sniffing the lemon-scented air, Carly wrinkled her nose and broke into a run. She didn't stop running until the lemon orchards were behind her.

On her left now was a steep wooded rise and on her right a long expanse of paintless picket fence. Beyond the fence straggly rows of tombstones rose and fell over the rolling foothills of the Mupu Ridge range. Here and there larger marble monuments surrounded by low iron fences marked the burial plots of many Santa Luisa families.

When Carly reached the main entrance to the cemetery, she stopped. With one hand on the sagging gate she turned to look toward the west. The sun was low now, a fiery ball drifting in a red-gold sea of clouds. She pushed open the gate and began to run.

The cemetery road went straight down a long corridor between a double row of eucalyptus trees and then branched off in several directions. At the first branch Carly turned to the left and went on running, down a narrow path that wound between spreading live-oaks. A few yards farther on she came to a sudden stop at a low iron fence. Breathing hard, she squatted down in the dry grass and waited for her heart to slow—and for the soft, sad mystery to begin.

It was a large plot, one of the largest in the graveyard, but most of its surface was smooth and bare except for dry dead weeds and here and there the scattered remains of withered bouquets. A stranger walking by would at first notice only one tombstone, a tall, slim obelisk of granite. From where she crouched outside the fence, Carly could read the inscription on one side of its broad rectangular base:

Edward Clark Carlton
born China, Maine, 1827
died Santa Luisa, California 1894

And on the other side:

Mehitabel Johnson Carlton
born China, Maine, 1836

Below that was the blank space that would not be filled in until Aunt M. was dead, too, and buried beside her husband.

Shifting her position, Carly turned to her left where the Carlton plot bordered the Mupu Creek with its edging of willows and cottonwoods. There in the deep shade, where the willow branches bent softly like the limp limbs of weeping mourners, was Petey's grave.

The tombstone was a small slab of marble with a rounded top on which was carved the likeness of a sleeping lamb. Beneath the lamb, in large letters, were three words, OUR LITTLE LAMB, and below that in smaller letters:

Peter Hartwick
born March 1893
died July 1895

The grass on the small mound was faintly green.

Carly sighed deeply. Then she stepped over the fence and made her way along the narrow path that her feet had long since worn through the tall dead grass. At the end of the path she sat down on Petey's grave and got ready to cry.

❧❀❀ *chapter 6*

She always cried at Petey's grave. All she had to do was to read his name and the two dates, just two short years apart, and a lump would fill her throat. Sometimes when, as now, the long, dry months had turned the grass on all the other graves a dull uniform brown, she would also look at the green of the small mound and say, "The green grave, watered by tears, watered by bitter tears." Then she would throw herself down across the grave and say, "Our little lamb," over and over again until tears overflowed her eyes and fell down to sink into the earth. When the crying was over, she usually rolled over on her back and lay for a while looking up through the willow branches and thinking about death and eternity and other sad, mysterious things.

Sometimes she thought about other deaths she had cried over in the past—Little Eva's, Beth's in *Little Women*, and, of course, Beautiful Joe's. They were all so beautifully, terribly sad, and yet they didn't always make her cry, at least not anymore. The first few times she'd read them, of course, she had wept and wept, but after a while those deaths had less effect, even Beautiful Joe's, over whose sad end she once had cried until she had nearly drowned in her own tears. But it was only for Petey's death that she could always cry. Which was a mystery in itself, really, since poor little Petey had actually died a year before she was born.

On the other hand, however, he had been her own brother and he had lived and died among people she knew, and she had heard so much about him—about the beautiful, brilliant, good little boy who had died so young. Every member of the family had special Petey stories, except perhaps for Lila, who had only been four years old when Petey died. Carly knew all the stories by heart. She remembered the ones that were especially Aunt M.'s, or Nellie's or Charles's or Father's, and, of course, the ones that Mama told. Many of the Petey stories were especially Mama's, because she talked about him so much. Everyone said that she still hadn't recovered from Petey's death, and some people said she never would.

Of course, Mama had not been strong even before the Hartwicks left their home in Maine. Father said that Mama's lungs had always been weak. She'd had pneumonia twice and the doctor said she would not live through a third time. That, Father said, was the main reason he had decided to accept Aunt Mehitabel's invitation to come to California. He had hoped the mild weather would improve Mama's health. But, mild weather or not, Mama hadn't wanted to come.

Everyone knew that Anna Hartwick hadn't wanted to leave her birthplace in the state of Maine and her relatives and friends. Sometimes she even wrote poetry about it—poems about autumn colors and snow and being homesick and far from home. But she had agreed to come for the sake of her husband and family. "Ezra really needed to make a new start," Carly had heard her say more than once. "He should never have tried to be an educator. He lacked the patience and forbearance. We really had no choice but to accept Aunt

Mehitabel's offer." So Anna had agreed to leave her birth-place and, with five young children, travel three thousand miles to a strange new world. "Charles, my eldest," Mama told people, "was nine when we arrived in Santa Luisa and my baby—Petey, my baby—was only two." "Only two," she would say again, and her beautiful eyes would fill with tears.

When the Hartwicks first arrived in Santa Luisa, they all lived at Greenwood with Aunt M., because the house on the ranch was being rebuilt. The ranch house had once been Edward Carlton's home, but when he married Aunt M., they moved to Greenwood, and the old house had been used by a foreman's family. Later on it became a dormitory for seasonal workers, and by the time the Hartwicks arrived it was run-down. So all the Hartwicks had to stay with Aunt M. at Greenwood while the ranch house was being repaired—and while they were still there Petey had suddenly sickened and died.

"Eighteen ninety-five," Carly whispered, and reached up above her head to touch the sharp-edged furrows where the date was carved into the marble tombstone. Then she rolled over onto her stomach and rested her chin in her hands. Staring at the inscription, she wondered how a date, one short day between sunrise and sunset, could bring something so final and endless as death, a death that ended one life and changed so many others, forever and ever.

"When that baby died," Aunt M. had often told her, "your mother went into a serious decline. Brain fever, Dr. West called it, though there were others who diagnosed it differently. Took to her room and didn't come out for more than six months. Your father, poor man, did what he could, but he had the ranch to manage and a thousand and one things to learn about farming in California. And then there were the children. Four lively children here at Greenwood for all that time. Charles and Nellie were good as gold, of course. Always have been. Too good, to my way of thinking. But Arthur and Lila were a different matter entirely."

"Lila wasn't bad, was she?" Carly asked. She didn't have to ask about Arthur. Arthur, she knew, had never been particularly good. Even Nellie, who had always been partial to Arthur, wouldn't go so far as to say that he had ever been what you might call good. But Lila? "What did Lila do when she lived with you?" Carly had asked Aunt M.

"Whatever she wanted to," Aunt M. said, but then she had looked at Carly and smiled. "Don't look so shocked, child," she said. "Your beloved Lila wasn't really a naughty little girl. She always minded her manners and did what she was told. As long as you were looking, at least. But she always got her way in the long run. And when she really wanted something, she always got it. You could count on that."

"And what about me?" Carly had asked, grinning. "How bad was I?"

"Terrible," Aunt M. said. "A holy terror." Then she smiled and hugged Carly and kissed her on top of the head. "You were the most beautiful baby in the world," she said, "from the first day you were born—from the first minute. I was the first one to hold you, you know."

Carly knew. She'd heard about it many times. How her birth had not been the cure for her mother's deep depression, as everyone had hoped it would be, and instead had nearly resulted in her death. So Aunt M. had been the first one to hold Carly, and afterward when Mama was sick for so long there had been no one to take care of the new baby except Aunt M. "And Woo Ying," Carly said. "Woo Ying took care of me too."

Aunt M. snorted. "Took care of you!" she said. "Smothered you, would be more like it. Spoiled you within an inch of your life. Wouldn't let you cry for a moment. Would have carried you around under his arm every minute you were awake, if I'd let him. For six months that crazy old Chinaman cleaned house, and stirred the soup, and fed the chickens with one arm, with you tucked under the other like a little sack of rice. It's a wonder you lived through it."

Thinking of herself as a sack of rice under Woo Ying's arm made Carly giggle—and the sound echoed startlingly in the silence of the graveyard. She sat up suddenly, wiping the last of the tears for Petey off her cheeks, and then scrambled to her feet. It was almost dark.

Grabbing the bottle she kept hidden in the fence corner, Carly vaulted the fence, pushed through the hanging willow branches, and slid down the steep slope to the creek. While she waited for the bottle to fill, she glanced around nervously at the pockets of changing, wavering darkness under the overhanging trees, shaking the bottle to make it fill more quickly and scolding herself under her breath. Crazy to lie there daydreaming, in a graveyard, of all places. Crazy to get home so late and worry everybody. Nellie was going to be so angry.

"Dunce, blockhead, ninny," she told herself as she scrambled back up the embankment. "Hurry, hurry, hurry." She stopped just long enough to empty the bottle over Petey's grave—because bitter tears needed a little help in such hot weather—snatched up her package, and headed for home at a run.

Running was a mistake. Walking in a dark graveyard would have been bad enough, but running was an invitation to panic. As Carly's feet slipped and stumbled over the uneven surface of the dirt road, dark shadows and misty shapes oozed out of hidden places and slid toward her. A few yards before the gate she slipped and fell, tearing her stocking and skinning her left knee and the palms of both hands. Almost before the pain had time to begin she was on her feet and running again; a limping run that took her as far as the gate before she turned back to retrieve her package—because even graveyard ghosts and a bloody knee weren't going to make her forget a new book that was probably too stimulating.

When Carly got home that night it was dark. Her face was dirty, and blood from her skinned knee had run clear down to her ankle. Nellie was waiting on the veranda, and just as Carly had feared, she was extremely worried and angry. And then, just as she was beginning to calm down, Carly had to go and make it worse by saying that it was a good thing Father wasn't at home.

Nellie was cleaning Carly's skinned knee with Sears, Roebuck Microbe Killer and she stopped suddenly and narrowed her eyes. Carly realized immediately that she'd made a mistake.

"And just what do you mean by that, young lady?" Nellie said.

So Carly quickly said she didn't mean anything and Nellie said that if she was trying to imply that Father was too strict, or unfair, or unkind, it just went to show what an ungrateful, unnatural child she really was, because Father was a wonderful parent, strict—yes—but no more than necessary, and she just wished that he had been here tonight to see how thoughtless and careless his youngest daughter could be.

She'd been dabbing at Carly's knee while she was talking, and for a long time Carly didn't say anything except "Ouch" and "Be careful, Nellie," and by the time the knee and Nellie's tirade were finally finished she was crying a little.

"I'm sorry, Nellie. I'm sorry," she said, fanning her smarting knee with both hands. "It hurts, Nellie. It hurts a lot."

"It has to hurt to do any good," Nellie said curtly, but then her voice softened and she said, "It won't hurt for long. You run along out to the kitchen and eat something. I put a plate in the warming oven for you."

Later, while Carly was eating at the kitchen table, Nellie came in and got out the milk pans and began skimming the cream into the churn.

"I'll do that," Carly said. "I'll do the churning in the morning." She wanted to do something for Nellie to make up for worrying her, and besides, churning was her favorite chore, since it could be done while reading.

Nellie smiled. "All right. In the morning." She picked up Carly's empty plate and took it to the sink. "You run along to bed now."

Carly hobbled to the door. Then she stopped and said, "I'm sorry I worried you, Nellie. Was Mama worried too? Did she ask where I was?"

Nellie put down the milk pan she was drying and looked at it for a moment before she came over to Carly and put an arm around her shoulders.

"No," she said. "She didn't ask. And I didn't mention it to her. She's had such bad dizzy spells lately, and if she worries, it always brings one on." She smiled and gave Carly's shoulders a little squeeze. "I suppose she thought you were staying over at Aunt M.'s."

Carly squeezed back. "I suppose so," she said.

❀❀❀❀ *chapter* 7

It was a little before noon when Carly burst through the back door at a dead run and leapt the three steps to the ground without breaking her stride. She was racing down the well-worn path at breakneck speed when suddenly she grabbed at her waist and came to a skidding, stumbling stop. Her trousers were falling off. Hitching up her skirt, she pulled up the tweed knickers she was wearing under her dress and, clutching them tightly, was back at top speed in an instant. A practiced skid around the honeysuckle trellis that hid the outhouse from public view, and she had reached her destination.

It wasn't until the emergency was over that it occurred to her to wonder if anyone had been watching. If Father had seen her, or anyone who might tattle to Father, she was in trouble. And it would be her own fault. She'd been told often enough that it was not only unladylike, but also positively indecent, to wait so long that you had to run. But she wasn't the only one to blame.

Peering around the trellis, Carly rehearsed all the reasons it wasn't entirely her fault, just in case Father was in the backyard and had seen her making an indecent spectacle of herself. First of all it was Father himself who insisted that the outhouse had to be so far away from everything and so well hidden. Nobody else, she was sure, had so far to walk—or run, in extreme emergencies—through a maze of concealing hedges and trellises.

But most of all, of course, it was Alfred Quigley's fault. It was his fault because if he hadn't cost Aunt M. and Father so much money, they would have been able to afford a modern toilet at the ranch house a long time ago—a lovely indoor toilet with a pull-chain flush just like the one at Greenwood, instead of an unsanitary old two-seater clear across the backyard.

Carly heaved an indignant sigh and ventured out from behind the honeysuckles. The backyard appeared to be deserted. Relieved, she started up the path at a fast skip, when a sudden sound brought her to a stop. Someone had giggled.

The sound was familiar. "Matt?" Carly called softly. "Where are you? Come on out. I know it's you."

Something stirred behind the branches of the thick hedge next to the toolshed, and a moment later the long droopy ears and the shaggy gray-brown head of an old donkey appeared. The donkey regarded Carly sadly and then reached down to nibble at a handy spear of grass. There followed the thud of bare heels on well-padded ribs, but the donkey only dropped his head lower as he stretched his neck toward a larger patch of dry weeds. The thuds turned into a rapid tattoo, the donkey grunted loudly and shuffled forward, and his rider came into view—a small boy with dark, curly hair and lively gray-green eyes. It was Matt, all right.

Ever since Carly had come to live at the ranch house she and Matt had played and fought, and rode donkeys and explored for gold and built treehouses together. Back when they'd been first and second graders they'd even played together sometimes at school. They didn't do that anymore because boys and girls their age never did at Santa Luisa Grammar School. But at home, in Hamilton Valley, they still had fun together—when they weren't fighting.

"Did you make it?" Matt said, grinning wickedly.

Carly glared. "Think you're funny, don't you?" She grabbed a switch off the peach tree and waved it threateningly.

"Hey, gee up. Gee up, Barney," Matt yelled, jerking up on the hackamore reins and pounding the donkey's ribs with his heels.

Barney snatched a last nibble of grass and shuffled forward, but Carly was faster. The switch was about to fall when Matt leapt off Barney's back and took shelter behind him. For a moment they faced each other over the shaggy back, Carly swishing her switch and Matt poised to leap back and away. Suddenly his gaze focused on Carly's legs. "Hey," he said. "What the Sam Hill you wearing?"

Carly looked down—and forgot about whacking the sass out of Matt Kelly. Dropping her switch, she leaned forward with her chin on Barney's back and motioned for him to come closer. "They're trousers," she whispered. "I've been playing Sherlock Holmes. You want to play?"

Matt eyed her suspiciously. "What kinda homes?" he said.

"Sherlock. Sherlock Holmes," Carly frowned impatiently. "The great detective. Don't you know about Sherlock Holmes? I borrowed a book about him from Aunt M., and it's the most exciting thing I ever read. I've been up in the attic making Sherlock Holmes costumes all morning and next I'm going to start detecting mysteries and crimes and things like that. Do you want to too? You can be Doctor Watson."

"I don't want to play. I'm no doctor," Matt said. "I want to go exploring. I thought we could go exploring on the ridge today. I brought some apples and venison jerky, and Rosemary too."

"Rosemary? Where?"

"Back there. Tied to the bushes."

Standing on tiptoes, Carly peered over Barney's back in the direction of Matt's point and caught a glimpse of another donkey, a smaller, trimmer, and much livelier donkey whose name was Rosemary. She'd almost forgotten that Matt had promised that she'd get to ride Rosemary the next time they went exploring. It was a hard decision to make—Rosemary or Sherlock Holmes. For two days now she'd had been preparing herself for a career as a detective, and she was almost ready to begin work on her first mystery. But, on the other hand, an exploration on donkeyback was hard to resist, particularly when it was her turn to ride Rosemary. Suddenly she had the solution.

"All right. We'll go exploring. And on the way we'll be Sherlock Holmes and Doctor Watson."

"Well," Matt began, frowning uncertainly, but Carly didn't wait to hear any more. "Wait a minute. I'll be right back," she called over her shoulder as she started for the house at a run. On the back porch she slipped out of the trousers, an outgrown pair of Arthur's which she had been trying on when it became necessary to leave the attic in a hurry. Stashing them behind a box of oranges, she opened the back door and stopped to listen. The kitchen was empty and the house seemed unusually silent. Where had everyone gone?

That morning at breakfast Carly's mind had been so full of Sherlock Holmes that she'd neglected to listen to everyone else's plans, but she knew that Mama, at least, would be at home. Mama, and one other person, since Mama was never left alone. Everything depended on who that other person might be, because while Mama almost never said no, she almost never said yes either. And there were some members of the family who were apt to say no to an exploring trip on the Kellys' donkeys.

Carly tiptoed through the dining room, and in the parlor she found Mama asleep on the sofa, and Charles sitting in the rocking chair reading a newspaper. Carly couldn't help smiling with relief. If Charles was taking care of Mama, it meant that no one else was at home.

Charles Emerson Hartwick, Carly's oldest brother, was twenty-one years old and a full-grown man, at least in size and appearance. But in many ways he seemed younger than Arthur. Carly supposed that was because Arthur was quick and daring and handsome, while Charles was slow and uncertain and stammered when he talked. Some people, particularly Father, said that Charles would try the patience of a saint, but Carly didn't think that was fair. If you didn't rush him, Charles did all right with words, and he did even better with his hands. Carly's play house and Tiger's beautiful doghouse had been built by Charles.

Sometimes strangers said Charles was exactly like Father, and they did look something alike, tall and pale with gray eyes and stiff heavy hair the color of summer grass. But in nearly every other way Charles and Father couldn't have been more different. For instance, when it came to getting permission to do almost anything, Father was probably the worst person in the world to have to ask, and Charles was pretty nearly the best. Carly tiptoed across the room and whispered in Charles's ear.

"Where's Father?"

"Apricot orchard," Charles said without taking his eyes off the paper.

"Where's Nellie?"

"Sh-sh-shopping." Perhaps because of his stammer, Charles never said more than was absolutely necessary.

"And Lila?"

Charles nodded. "W-w-went too."

Carly grinned. "May I go donkey riding with Matt?" she asked.

Charles had gone back to his paper. Carly poked him and whispered her request a little bit louder.

"Hmm. B-b-better ask Mama."

"But she's asleep. I don't think we should wake her. Do you?"

Charles raised his head enough to peer over the top of his newspaper. He stared at Mama for several seconds and then for several more seconds he nodded his head. "G-g-guess not," he said at last, and went back to his paper.

Carly decided that was as close to a yes as was necessary, and tiptoed discreetly out of the room. A quick trip to the attic and then a detour into the pantry and she had collected everything she needed and stashed it all in a deep pouch formed by the bunched-up skirt of her pinafore. Then she flew out the back door for the second time within ten minutes.

No one was in the backyard, but a lot of excited barking was coming from behind the toolshed. Matt waited there because, like most people, he was scared of Father, and ordinarily it was a good hiding place. But not if Tiger was around, because he knew donkeys meant that somebody was going somewhere, and of course he wanted to go too. Tiger loved going places. Arthur said it was a good thing dogs didn't have souls, because Tiger would have traded his in for a good walk any day of the year.

"All right, Tiger, you can go," Carly told him, and he immediately began to celebrate by running around and around the donkeys at top speed with his tail tucked between his legs. Tiger always ran in circles when he was excited, going so fast that his whole body sloped in toward the center of the circle, like a flying bird tilting into a turn. Rosemary watched him nervously as he circled past, her head flipping from side to side, but Barney only blinked sleepily every time the four-legged comet orbited past his nose. Dodging to avoid being run down, Carly yelled, "Stop it! Stop that this minute, you crazy dog." Tiger went on running.

Safely inside Tiger's racetrack, she fished around in her pinafore pouch and brought out two bags. "Cookies," she said, dropping them into the saddlebags that hung across Barney's shaggy back. "And oranges."

Matt peered into the still bulging pouch formed by Carly's pinafore. "What else you got in there?" he asked.

"Costumes," Carly said. "This one's for you." She pulled out a black felt hat and handed it to Matt. It had been a ladies' hat once, but with its veil and flowers removed it looked quite a bit like a gentleman's derby. As Matt examined it doubtfully, she produced a boy's school-cap that she had reupholstered with a plaid material. "And this one is a deerstalker's cap, like Sherlock wears. I've got other stuff too—trousers and coats and vests—but the donkeys would get it all dirty. So we'll just wear the hats today. Okay?"

Matt argued, protesting that he didn't want to wear no ladies' hat, but after Carly assured him that it looked just like the one Dr. Watson was wearing in the illustration in "The Adventure of the Speckled Band," he finally gave in.

"Well, all right, but I'm giving you fair warning—if we meet anybody, I'm going to sit on it," he muttered as he tried to tug Barney's head up out of the grass patch. Then he noticed what Carly was doing. "Lordy, Carly," he said in a screeching whisper. "What are you doing now?"

"What does it look like I'm doing?" Carly said. "I'm taking off my shoes and stockings."

"Why?" Matt wailed. "We got to get going."

Like a lot of Matt's "whys," that was one Carly didn't intend to answer. It ought to be obvious. Riding bareback on a donkey was a hairy, sweaty business, and legs were a lot easier to wash than white stockings. But to explain that, one would have to use the word *legs*, which, of course, was not a proper thing to say in mixed company.

"Why not?" she said as she tucked the stockings into her shoes and hid them in the hedge. "You're barefoot."

"Yeah, but you're a girl."

That was a sore point. Carly had been through dozens of arguments about why boys got to go barefoot all summer and girls, at least girls in the Hartwick family, never did. Giving Matt her version of the glare that Arthur called "Father's bone-chiller," she jumped up on her stomach across Rosemary's back, swung her leg over, and set off at a sharp trot.

"I'm not a girl," she called as she whizzed past, leaving Barney and Matt in a cloud of dust. "I'm Sherlock Holmes." She was nearly to where the Ridge Trail turned off from the Hamilton Valley Road before she slowed Rosemary down and let Barney catch up.

❧❊❧ *chapter 8*

At first the trail wound up through low, rolling foothills and
Carly and Matt were able to ride side by side—if Carly held
Rosemary in and Matt kept up a steady tattoo on Barney's
ribs. As the donkeys made their way slowly across dry creek
beds and between clumps of oaks and madrones, Tiger
scouted around them in a frenzy of excited sniffing, and Carly
tried to explain about Sherlock Holmes and the art of being a
detective.

"Like in 'The Adventure of the Blue Carbuncle,' " she
said, "—there's an old hat that a friend of Sherlock's found
with a goose—"

"The goose was wearing a hat?" Matt interrupted in a sarcastic tone of voice.

"No, ninny! Just be still and let me finish. The goose was
dead. Somebody had dropped it, along with the old hat, on
the sidewalk, and this friend brought them both to Sherlock
Holmes. And it turned out the goose had a precious jewel in
its craw, so Sherlock examined the hat to find out whose it
was. And just by examining the hat with a magnifying glass

he found out all kinds of things about the man who dropped it."

"Like what?"

"Well, guess. What do you think he found out?"

"Okay, I'll guess. Wait a minute. Lemme think."

Lost in thought, Matt forgot about kicking, and by the time he came up with an answer Barney had fallen several yards behind. Carly watched him over her shoulder.

"Okay. I got it," he yelled finally. "Pull up a minute."

Carly stopped Rosemary, and Matt thumped Barney's ribs so soundly that he broke into a bone-jarring trot. "Okay," Matt said proudly as he reined in, clutching his derby to keep it from flying off. "He knew how big the man's head was, and how rich he was, and if he had cooties. How's that?"

Carly smiled indulgently. "And," she said, "that he had been rich but now he was poor, and that he was a drunkard, and that he was pretty old, and what kind of hair tonic he used, and that he didn't have gaslight in his house even though most people in London did by then, and that his wife didn't love him anymore."

"Shucks," Matt said, "I don't believe that. Do you?"

"Sure I do. That was easy for Sherlock Holmes. All he had to do was observe, and that's what I'm going to learn how to do."

"Yeah?" Matt said. "Why?"

"Well," Carly said, "it's just that . . ." and then she stopped. She knew why. It was just hard to put into words. It was hard to explain why the idea of being able to look at things—simple, ordinary, everyday things—and be able to learn all kinds of secrets from them, was so terribly exciting. Exciting in some ways like being invisible would be exciting. Except that with being invisible you'd be able to see and hear everything because no one would know you were there. And with observing you could be right there, and people would

53

be trying to hide all the most interesting secrets from you, just like always, and you'd be able to read all the answers from simple ordinary objects—like from a dirty fingernail, or a bit of blotting paper, or an old felt hat.

"Look," Matt said suddenly, "there's my house. Did you know you could see our place from here?"

They were on the ridge trail by now, high up on the side of the mountain, and below them was Grizzly Flats. Dan Kelly, Matt's grandfather, had always dry-farmed wheat and barley in the high valley, when he wasn't off tramping around in the wilderness prospecting for gold. According to Aunt M., who'd been a friend of the Kellys' for years, he'd never found any gold and he'd not had much more luck with his farming. But he'd gone right on trying and he and his wife, Maggie, had raised their big family right there in the little house on the Flats. After their own children grew up and went away, Dan and Maggie were alone for a while, but then one of their daughters died and left a little motherless boy. So Matt had come to live with the Kellys, just about the time that Carly came to live with her own family at the ranch house.

Looking out over the Flats, Matt and Carly rested the donkeys and watched while far down below Maggie came out of the back door carrying a bucket and crossed the yard to the pigsty. After she went back into the house they went on up the steep, winding path toward the ridge.

By the time they finally reached the top, the donkeys were sweaty and winded again from the long climb. Matt and Barney had fallen behind, so Carly dismounted while she waited for them to catch up. Her legs felt a little bit stiff and achy, and very sticky. Reaching under her dress, she tugged at her underthings where they were stuck to her legs by donkey sweat. Then she shook first one leg and then the other and swished her skirt around to create a cooling breeze. Rosemary watched with a thoughtful expression on her pretty donkey face, and then she lowered her head and shook herself violently.

Carly scratched the shaggy, sweaty neck. "Poor Rosemary," she whispered into the long gray ear. "You're hot and tired too. Aren't you?" Rosemary turned and rested her chin on Carly's shoulder and puffed warm hay-scented breath across her face. "Okay," Carly told her. "We'll rest for a while."

"Let's have lunch here while the donkeys rest a little," she said as Barney plodded up alongside.

"Lunch," Matt said. "I thought we were going to eat at the spring. We got to have water. You can't eat much of Grandpa's jerky without something to drink."

"We'll have two lunches," Carly said. "We'll eat my lunch here and yours at the spring. All right?"

Matt shrugged.

It was nice on the crest. The wind was from the west and cooler, carrying a trace of ocean freshness, and the whole world seemed to be stretched out before them. Far below, in the center of the valley, sunlight glinted on the water that flowed down from Carlton Spring, while farther away to the south the rocky summit of the Mupu Hills rose up to meet the bright sky. Matt and Carly sat under a scraggly oak and sucked oranges and nibbled on cookies while the donkeys grazed around them, and Carly told Matt all about the Hound of the Baskervilles.

She'd just gotten to the scariest part when Tiger came circling back from his latest attempt to catch a jackrabbit and crashed through some bushes right behind them. They both jumped and Matt dropped the orange he was eating and then they began to laugh, because funny little old Tiger was such a long way from being a slavering, red-eyed hound. Tiger smelled the cookies and immediately decided to give up hunting in favor of begging. He went through all his tricks in rapid succession, sitting up, rolling over, and playing dead, while Matt and Carly tossed him bits of cookie. They were still giggling when suddenly Matt grabbed Carly's arm.

"Look!" he said, pointing out over the valley. "It's a condor."

An enormous bird, its huge black wings spread wide, was drifting down over the top of the Mupu Range directly toward the spot where they were sitting.

Grabbing Tiger, Carly dived into the bushes, but Matt sat still, staring as if in frozen fascination. A dark shadow swept over him and the air was suddenly full of a sound unlike anything Carly had ever heard, the dry rustling whisper of feathers in gigantic wings. Carly hid her face on Tiger's back, expecting to feel sharp talons clutching her, or hear Matt's screams as the condor carried him away. But nothing happened, and when she raised her head, fearfully, Matt was still there.

"Matt," Carly whispered as soon as she could find her voice, "Hide. It'll get you."

Matt took a deep breath and let it out slowly. "No, it won't," he said. "Look."

Carly turned loose the squirming Tiger and crawled to where she could peer out over the valley. The condor had turned northward and now it was gliding away from them toward the high mountains.

Carly gasped for air, and the hungry feeling in her lungs made her realize that she'd been forgetting to breathe. As the thudding of her heart began to ease, she slowly got to her feet to watch as the condor swept upward, glided over the mountain crest, and disappeared as suddenly as it had come.

❧❀❀ *chapter* 9

"How do you know they won't eat you?" Carly yelled as she crawled back into the bushes. She found her deerstalker cap hanging from a twig and backed out again to where Matt was waiting. "How do you know?" she said again. She put the cap on and pulled it down low on her forehead. "They're big enough to. Arthur says their wings are ten feet across."

Matt was grinning his evil grin.

"What are you laughing at?" Carly said threateningly.

Matt stepped back out of range. Then he shrugged and said, "You look a sight, in that crazy cap. And your face is dirty as sin."

She would probably have whacked him if her mind hadn't been so completely full of condors. She took off the cap and wiped her face with it and put it back on.

"I asked you," she said, "how you know so much about condors."

"My grandpa told me," Matt said. "He knows all about them. He says they only eat dead things. They might eat you if you were already dead, but they don't kill anything. They don't have the right kind of feet, or something. Killing birds have curved claws, like owls and eagles, and condors just have big old flat feet like a great big chicken. They're"—he thought for a minute, and then nodded—"scavengers. They're just scavengers, like buzzards, and like that."

Carly wasn't sure. "How come your grandpa knows so much about condors? Arthur says he knows all about them, and he told me they're really fierce and dangerous. He says they can carry away a half-grown calf."

Matt shook his head. "Naw! They can't. My grandpa knows. He knows because he prospected way up in the mountains back of Sespe Creek and he used to spend a lot of time watching condors. He says they're good things to have around and they don't kill anything. He'll be right pleased to hear we saw one. There used to be a lot more of them around here. Grandpa says they used to fly down this valley all the time on their way to the spring."

"The spring. You mean our spring? Carlton Spring?"

"Sure. That's why the old-timers called it Condor Spring. My grandpa still calls it that. Grandpa says that after the condors finished feeding, they used to go to the spring to drink and bathe themselves. He says he used to hide in the bushes and watch them kind of playing in the water like a bunch of overgrown blackbirds. And once he saw a couple of them doing a kind of dance-like, holding their wings way out and bobbing their heads up and down and shuffling their feet. I asked him why they did that and he laughed and said he guessed it was just kind of a condor hoedown."

Carly stared at Matt in astonishment. Condors, according to everything she'd ever heard, were horrible creatures, huge and black with bare red heads and fierce blood-red eyes, monsters capable of killing and carrying away good-sized animals and, in some of the stories, even smallish people. "My goodness, Matt," she said. "Sounds like your grandpa likes those awful things."

"My grandpa," Matt said, "says that condors are beautiful. He says there's not anything in the world can hold a candle to them when it comes to flying. He says he's seen one riding the wind for a whole hour, just soaring round and round over the hills, without having to flap its wings even one time."

Carly turned to look out over the deep valley. She knew Dan Kelly wasn't the kind to make up things that weren't true. For a moment she tried to imagine the condor as she had seen it gliding in over the Mupu Ridge. She wished she'd taken a better look instead of diving under the bushes the way she had. Looking up the valley toward where the great black bird had sunk out of sight below the horizon, she found herself wishing it would come back again. Suddenly she ran to where Rosemary was grazing and threw the hackamore reins up over her neck. "Come on," she yelled. "Let's get going. I want to see where the condors dance."

She had been to the Carlton Spring only once before, when Charles and Arthur had ridden up to clean out the spring pond. They'd taken Lila and Carly with them, because Arthur said it was a shame that they'd never even seen the spring that could put the whole family in the poorhouse if it dried up, or if old Quigley got his way. But her memory of it wasn't very clear. If she'd known then about the condors, she'd have paid much more attention.

From the crest above Grizzly Flats the trail wound in and out along hillsides that fell steeply down to Carlton Creek. Here and there it dipped to cross the beds of barrancas that in winter added to the creek's flow, but now in June were completely dry. And there were times when it was no more than a narrow ledge above sharp drops—dangerous, perhaps, to riders on mounts less surefooted than Barney and Rosemary.

But Carly wasn't thinking of the trail, or even of Sherlock Holmes. Her mind was full of condors now—there'd be time for Sherlock Holmes on the way home—and whenever the trail widened, she pulled up and waited to bombard Matt with a new batch of condor questions. And nearly always Matt had answers, fascinating answers.

She learned that the condor they'd seen was probably young—a fledgling, Matt called it—a fact that could be determined by the amount of white showing under the wings.

"Didn't you see the white?" Matt asked. "How it looked kind of speckled? Those places are bigger and pure white when they're full grown."

But she didn't learn if it had been a he or a she. "No way of telling," Matt said. "Not even up close."

But Matt was able to tell her that a mother condor lays only one egg every two or three years and that it takes almost a year for the baby to learn to fly, and even after that the parents feed it for a long time. "They're real good parents," Matt said. "They take good care of their babies and they don't fight or anything. Grandpa says human folks could learn a lot from condors about being good families."

Carly pulled Rosemary to a complete stop and, of course, Barney stopped too. Matt's eyes had a gleam to them, a shiny look like Father had when he quoted Ralph Waldo Emerson, or like Mama's eyes when she talked about Maine.

"Grandpa says," Matt said, "the condors have lived in California for thousands and thousands of years, and there used to be lots and lots of them, but if people don't stop killing them and stealing their eggs there won't be any left before too long. And that will be a bad thing for everybody."

"Why?" Carly asked. "Why will it be bad for everybody?"

Matt shrugged. "I don't know for sure. Grandpa says

maybe the condors are like a sign to California, like the ravens in the Tower of London are a sign. Grandpa says there's a foretelling that says 'Woe to England' when the ravens leave the Tower. And maybe it's 'Woe to California' if we kill off our condors."

"Woe to California," Carly whispered, staring at Matt in wonder and surprise. The sound of it made her shoulders rise in a sudden shiver. "How come you never told me before?" she said. "How come you never said anything about condors and how your grandpa knows all about them and everything?"

Matt thought for a moment before he answered. "I don't know. You never asked me, I guess." Then he grinned. "Besides, you usually do all the talking."

It wasn't a very polite thing for Matt to say, even if there was some truth in it, but Carly wasn't in the mood for an argument. Instead she only jerked up on the hackamore reins and urged Rosemary into a rapid trot. For the next half hour she maintained the pace, while behind her Matt kicked and yelled and occasionally managed to get Barney to trot too. The narrow trail twisted and turned across steep slopes covered with knee-high golden grasses, along the edges of rocky outcroppings and under clumps of oaks and sycamores. It wasn't until the spring was in sight, a gleam of dark water in the shade of sheltering trees, that she pulled up and waited.

"Do you think they'll be there?" she whispered as Barney plodded up beside Rosemary.

"The condors?" Matt sounded surprised. "Naw, I don't reckon so. Grandpa says they don't come into Carlton Valley much anymore. Too many hunters."

"But we saw one." Carly wasn't going to give up the exciting possibility so easily. "It was flying this way. It might be there, don't you think?"

"Naw," Matt said stubbornly.

Carly set her chin. "I bet there is," she said. "I bet there's a condor there." Without waiting for another "naw" she set Rosemary at the last slope that led down into the narrow valley, and as the donkey slid surefootedly down the steep incline, she kept her eyes peeled for the glint of sunlight on shiny black feathers. They had reached level ground and the spring was only a few yards away when she saw it, and her breath caught in her throat. There was indeed a condor at Carlton Spring, and for just a moment she thought it was dancing.

❧❀❧❀ *chapter 10*

Sunlight filtering through overhanging branches gleamed on black feathers where, only a few feet from the edge of the spring pool, a condor seemed to be crouching, its head held low and its enormous wings spread and trailing out on either side. The wings swayed slightly, the long finger feathers at their tips stirring the dust. Carly pulled Rosemary to a quick stop and sat motionless, her heart racing. Her attention was fixed so intently on the condor that it took her a moment to realize that Matt had slid off Barney and was approaching the spring. He was, in fact, only a few feet from the condor before Carly noticed him.

"Matt, stop," she hissed.

Matt turned toward her and the look on his face was so strange that she seemed to feel, rather than see, it—like something hitting her in the pit of the stomach. "Why?" Matt said, in a voice as un-Mattlike as the expression on his face. "It's dead."

"Dead?" Carly stared at the condor in horror. It couldn't be dead. She'd seen it move. She slid off Rosemary and scrambled down to where Matt was waiting. Then, together, they approached the enormous black bird. Matt was right. It was dead.

There was a sign near the pool. Father had painted the sign and Arthur and Charles had mounted it on a sturdy pole on the day that Carly had first visited the spring. The sign said, NO TRESPASSING. THIS SPRING AND THE WATER IT PRODUCES IS THE PROPERTY OF THE CARLTON RANCH. But obviously someone had trespassed at the spring, and had left the body of a dead condor hanging across the sign.

Carly walked around the dead bird slowly, staring in horrified fascination. Its huge wings had been extended along the length of the signboard and then allowed to trail downward, where they swayed slightly as the wide feathers caught the wind. The broad tail and long reddish legs hung almost to the earth, and on the far side of the sign the huge red head with its fierce gray beak dangled limply. There was blood on the beak, and beneath it, on the ground, the blood had dripped down to form a small pool. As Carly walked around and around the carcass, Matt crouched in front of it, staring.

"Do you think it's the one we saw flying?" Carly whispered.

Matt reached out and lifted a wing and put it back down. Then he ran his hand through the feathers on the hunched shoulders.

"Naw, couldn't be. This one's been dead for at least a day or two. Somebody shot it when it came in to drink, and after it was dead they hung it across the sign thataway. Come on. Help me get it down."

Matt took one wing and Carly took the other and together they lifted the condor off the sign, and spread it out on the ground. Stretched out that way, the span of its great dark wings was almost unbelievable. Just one of the wings was longer than Matt was tall.

Tiger, who'd been keeping a safe distance while the condor was still on the signpost, came up then, growling bravely. He sniffed all around the body with the hair up on his shoulders, acting fierce and kind of proud, as if he'd killed it himself. He might have started worrying it or even rolling on it —Tiger always rolled on dead things if he got a chance—but Matt and Carly chased him away.

Just about then Matt remembered his venison and apples, but when he got them out of the saddlebag Carly said she wasn't hungry.

"That so?" Matt said. "First time I ever heard of you not being hungry."

"Well, I'm not now," Carly said crossly. She went over to Rosemary and leaned her face against the donkey's neck. She didn't want to look at the condor's poor bloody body anymore. Looking at it while Matt crunched on an apple made her stomach do unpleasant things. And besides, it was time they were starting home.

"We ought to start back," she said. "Father might be home early tonight, and I don't want to be late."

Matt didn't argue. He stuck a piece of venison into his mouth, threw another piece to Tiger, and climbed up on Barney. "Let's go, then," he said, jerking Barney's head up out of the green spring-watered grass. "I sure don't want to take a chance on meeting up with your pa."

The sun was already out of sight behind the ridge and the shadows that filled the valley floor were creeping up the slope toward them, as they started off up the trail. They rode in silence until they reached the summit of Grizzly Ridge, but when they stopped for a minute to breathe the donkeys, Matt started asking questions about the spring and why the Quigleys claimed it was partly theirs.

Carly sighed. She wanted to go on thinking about condors. And besides, the spring problem was hard to explain. Particu-

65

larly since everybody in the family, including Aunt M. and Woo Ying, had a different way of explaining it, and they all got a little bit mixed up in Carly's mind when she tried to sort it out.

"Well," she said, hesitantly, "when my great-uncle, Edward Carlton, first came to California, he and Mr. Quigley were partners. They each owned their own land, but they shared a lot of things like a mill and a warehouse. And even though the spring was on Uncle Edward's property, they shared the water from that too. There wasn't any water company then and the spring was just about the only water there was. And Uncle Edward signed some kind of paper that said that he'd always share the water with Mr. Quigley. Only Aunt Mehitabel says what the writing on the paper meant was that they'd share all the water they had, not just the spring."

"But there's not enough of it," Matt said. "You couldn't irrigate all the Carlton and Quigley land from just that little old spring."

"No. I guess not. At least not if you grew things like citrus trees. But in the early days they only grew winter wheat, and olives and cattle—things that don't need much water. But then when Uncle Edward died old Alfred Quigley decided that Aunt M. should sell all of her land to him, only she didn't want to."

"Yeah, I heard about that," Matt said, grinning. "My grandpa says that old A. B. Quigley wasn't used to being told no, particularly by a little old lady. Grandpa laughs about how Mrs. Carlton told old Quigley a thing or two."

"Yes." Carly grinned too. She'd heard about what Aunt M. had said to old Quigley, and how angry it had made him. But then she sobered. "Old Quigley got the last laugh, I guess. Because after that he started the Santa Luisa Water Company and they got lots of water from wells and the river, and now all the people who belong to the company have lots of water, but the Quigleys won't let my aunt or my father belong, so all we have is the spring, and that's not enough to start citrus orchards. So my papa has to go on raising things that don't make much money and at the same time paying lawyers to keep old Quigley from taking away half of our spring water too."

"Quigley's a bad'un," Matt said, shaking his head.

"Quigley's a . . ." Carly could think of a word or two that she'd overheard Arthur using, but not being too sure what they meant, she decided against it. Instead she only said, "Aiii!" under her breath and kicked poor Rosemary a little harder than necessary.

They were almost to the ranch house and Carly was thinking mostly about how late it was and if she was going to be in trouble, when Matt suddenly pulled up alongside and said, "It was Henry and Bucky that done it."

"Done—did what?" Carly asked.

"Shot the condor."

Carly stared in amazement. "Henry? Henry Babcock? And Bucky?" Bucky Hansen was Henry's best friend and the second meanest boy in Santa Luisa.

"Sure," Matt said. "Who else? Old Henry Quigley Babcock."

"What makes you think it was Henry?" Carly asked.

"Well, first off, somebody tried to scratch off where it says Carlton Ranch on that there sign your pa put up. With a knife or something. You notice that? The way I figure, nobody'd do that but a Quigley."

Carly nodded her head. She'd been too busy looking at the poor dead condor. It did sound like a Quigley trick, and Alfred Bennington Quigley's brat of a grandson was certainly a likely suspect. Still, there were other Quigley friends and relatives who might have tried to ruin Father's sign. "But how do you know it was Henry?"

"Well, Henry has a new rifle. Got it for his birthday not long before school was out and bragged about it for days. About how he and Bucky were going hunting and all the critters they were going to kill. And besides, whoever did it was using those ferns over to the west side of the pond to hide in like it was a blind, or something. The ground was all scuffed up and there was a wrapper for a jawbreaker near where they'd been waiting. And what's more, they was playing mumblety-peg. I saw the knife marks. Don't know of any other Quigley who eats jawbreakers and plays mumblety-peg. Do you?"

"Matt!" Carly said. "That is wonderful. That is absolutely wonderful."

Matt looked suspicious. "What's wonderful?"

"The way you detected all those clues. Just exactly like Sherlock Holmes."

"That wasn't detecting. It was reading signs—like the Indians do. An old Indian friend of Grandpa's learned him how to do it, and he's been learning me ever since I was a baby."

"Well, I still think it's wonderful." Carly said. "I think . . ." What she was thinking was that she ought to promise Matt that the next time they played he could be Sherlock Holmes, but she really didn't want to. Not with her costume almost finished and everything. Suddenly she had an inspiration. "What was your Grandpa's Indian friend's name?" she said.

"Eenzie," Matt said. "That's what Grandpa called him, anyways. Said he couldn't get his mouth around his real Indian name."

"All right—Eenzie. The next time we play detective you can be Eenzie. Sherlock Holmes and Eenzie."

Matt didn't say anything. He just handed her the Dr. Watson hat with a big grin. Carly gave him Rosemary's reins, slid to the ground—and nearly collapsed. Her legs felt like they'd been permanently curved to fit a donkey's back, and straightening them hurt like fury. "Aiii," she said under her breath, as she pulled her shoes and stockings out of the hedge and started for the house at a stiff bowlegged run.

❧❀ *chapter 11*

"Carly! God in heaven, where have you been? What happened to you?" Nellie whispered fiercely. Her fingers dug into Carly's shoulders and her eyes darted frantically from Carly's bedraggled hair to her bare and dirty feet.

Following Nellie's gaze, Carly looked down at herself. She was terribly dirty, there was no doubt about that, and barefooted. But nothing worse than that. She'd almost expected, from the look on Nellie's face, to see a bloody wound or something else as horrible. "Nothing," she began. "Nothing happened. I just went donkey riding with Matt. I told Charles I was going. I—"

"Shhh!" Nellie's fingers dug deeper and she shook Carly like Tiger shaking a rat. "Get upstairs and clean up," she whispered between her teeth. "And hurry. Dinner's almost ready. I'll talk to you later, young lady." She grabbed Carly's wrist, pulled her into the hall, and shoved her toward the stairs. "Hurry," she whispered, "and be quiet. I'll send Lila up to help."

Carly didn't ask questions. She knew what the problem

was. The problem was Father, and what he would do and say if he knew that she had gone donkey riding and come home late—and dirty—and barefooted. But he didn't know. Not yet, anyway. Dashing up the stairs on silent bare feet, Carly sped down the hall to her room.

In less than a minute she was out of her dress and pinafore and had poured the contents of the water pitcher into the wide china basin. In her camisole and petticoat, she dipped a washcloth into the cold water and scrubbed her face, neck, and arms. Then she lifted the heavy basin to the floor and put one filthy foot into the water while she ran the washcloth up and down her leg. The other foot followed and she was drying frantically when Lila arrived.

Lila's anger was as unlike Nellie's as was everything else about Carly's two sisters. While Nellie's anger sizzled and spattered like frying bacon, Lila's glowed deep and silent as coals; deep and silent and beautiful, with a fiery sparkle in her wide eyes, and the frowning tilt of her eyebrows only emphasizing their perfect arch. Gliding to the closet, she snatched out Carly's blue dress with the sailor collar.

"Hold up your arms, you little . . ." Lila's voice was a sleek, silky threat. She jerked the dress over Carly's head and began to button it up the back. "You selfish, spoiled little monster. Sit down here on the stool and I'll brush your hair while you button your shoes."

Tears filled Carly's eyes. Real tears, now, from real hurt. Hurt that came from the coldness of Lila's voice as well as from the rough whacking of the stiff brush bristles against her scalp. "Ouch," she whispered, and turned her head to let Lila see the tears. But it didn't help. In fact, it only made matters worse.

"Don't try that old trick," Lila muttered. "And stop it! Right now! If your eyes are all red he'll want to know why. And then the rest of us will have to blacken our souls lying

71

for you, like always, while you just sit there, not caring. *Not caring,"* she said again, giving Carly's hair a final whacking brush before she retied the ribbon that pulled it back from her face. Then she turned her around roughly and stared at her. "There," she said, starting for the door. "You'll do. Now hurry."

"Wait, Lila. Don't be mad," Carly began, but Lila was gone.

Father was helping Mama into her chair when Carly arrived in the dining room. Bowls and platters of steaming food were already on the table, and Charles and Arthur and Lila were standing behind their chairs. Standing because, at the Hartwicks' table, everyone but Mama stood until after the blessing. As she moved quickly to her own place, Carly's eyes flicked across faces, trying, as she always did, to read the secrets that hid behind eyes and lips.

Father first. One always looked for Father's secrets first, knowing that they would not stay hidden for long, and that it sometimes helped to be prepared for their sudden revelation. One looked for narrowed eyes and twitching eyebrows, and sometimes a particular kind of smile. Carly watched as he bent over Mama, pushing in her chair, and then straightened to look quickly around the table. He was a tall man, and something about the way he always seemed to be looking down from a high place made him seem even taller. Head up and back, his quick gray eyes moved, without stopping, from face to face. Carly stifled a sigh of relief. At least there was no eagle-eyed, bone-chilling pause on her, or Nellie, or anyone else. Moving to the other end of the table, he took his place behind his high-backed chair.

Lila was next to Father. Her face was the hardest to read, as if her beauty formed so smooth a film that even fear or anger found little foothold there. Only the quickness with which her eyes turned away from Carly's told that she was still angry. If she saw Carly's humble don't-be-mad-at-me smile, she gave no sign.

Arthur's lopsided, almost invisible grin, as usual, seemed to be making fun of something, and when Carly caught his glance he lifted an eyebrow and gave his head the tiniest beginning of a shake. The shake perhaps meant, *Look out, you're in trouble,* or *We're all in trouble,* or maybe even *Good for you, Carly. You're the only one in this whole family with an ounce of spunk,* which was something he'd said to her more than once.

If anyone was acting strangely, it was Charles. His chair was next to Carly's, and as she looked up at him, his tense, nervous glance flickered around her without acknowledging her presence. It was like Charles to look without really seeing, but it was not like him to see and pretend not to. It seemed that Charles was angry too.

And back to Mama, pale and distant, her shoulders hunched as if in pain, her eyes already lowered for the blessing. She showed no sign of knowing that her youngest daughter was in trouble again. Nellie wouldn't have told her —not unless she had asked, and it wasn't likely that she had.

Then Nellie came in from the kitchen with the milk pitcher, and when she had taken her place they all bowed their heads. Silence. Silent waiting, waiting to hear who would give the blessing. Carly didn't really think she'd be the one. Father didn't call on her very often. But just in case, she got ready, rehearsing in her mind the words to a new one she'd recently learned in Sunday School, because Father didn't approve of always saying the same one.

"Thank you for this food we share," she murmured silently. "Thank you for your daily care. Thank you—"

"Charles."

Father often picked Charles. Perhaps because he was oldest, or perhaps because he never seemed to be prepared. As always, he stumbled and stuttered through the Lord's Prayer and then the "Bless this food to our use."

"Amen," Father said. The rest of the family echoed, "Amen," chairs scraped, and everyone sat down.

❧❀❀ *chapter* 12

Carly sighed with relief and inhaled a wonderful medley of smells: roast beef, gravy, mashed potatoes, and carrots and peas. She was, she realized suddenly, absolutely famished. The potatoes were next to her plate and she picked them up and sniffed appreciatively. She loved potatoes.

"Ha-rumm." The familiar rasping sound that meant that Father was about to speak froze the food-passing process all around the table. Swallowing the hungry juices that were filling her mouth, Carly, like the others, turned to the head of the table. Father was carving the roast beef. "Ha-rumm," he said again, and then, "Charles. One always rejoices in the familiar beauty of the Lord's Prayer. But it does seem that piety could be less monotonous. Would it be too much to ask that you favor us with a bit more variety in the future?"

Without turning her head Carly rolled her eyes toward her oldest brother. Charles's secrets were never well hidden—a sudden start followed by nervous embarrassment. "Yes, s-s-sir," he said. "I mean, no, sir. W-w-what prayer do you want me to s-s-say?"

Father's smile was dangerously jovial. "That's one decision I should think you would like to make for yourself, my boy. I should think that would be between you and the Almighty." The smile disappeared and Father turned to hand the platter of neatly carved beef to Lila. "Here you are, my girl. A fine roast. My compliments to our two lovely cooks."

Lila helped herself to the meat, and all around the table the passing process began again. Carly, almost dizzy from hunger, swallowed again and reluctantly passed the potatoes on to Charles, obeying the rule that when you started a dish you did not help yourself first unless it was offered back to you. She was afraid that poor Charles was in no condition to remember such polite niceties. Sure enough, still red-faced and blank-eyed, he simply spooned out a large helping and passed it on. Carly watched wistfully as the bowl started its long journey around the table. The best part, the middle of the white mound enriched by the deep well of yellow butter, would be gone by the time it came back to her.

"Nellie," Father said, "how did the shopping go? Were you able to get everything?"

Nellie's face was still flushed, either from the heat of the kitchen or from anger. "Yes, Father," she said quickly. "Everything but the axle grease. Mr. Stone was all out, but he says he'll be getting some more next month."

"Confound the man." Father's voice rang with anger, a sound that tightened lips and tensed muscles all around the table. "Shorting himself of grease in the middle of summer. A man as shortsighted as Abner Stone has no business trying to run a merchandising establishment."

A possible solution to the axle-grease problem occurred to Carly and she bounced excitedly. "Father," she said, "Father, I think—"

"Don't interrupt, Carly," Nellie said quickly.

Father seemed to have heard neither Carly nor Nellie. But

his frown seemed even more threatening as he continued, "If I'd thought for a minute that Stone's would be out of grease, I could have gotten some in Ventura. I wish to God—"

Lowering her voice Carly stubbornly tried again: "Father."

His eyes turned to Carly and all the Abner Stone–axle-grease anger seemed about to break on her head. "What is it?" he asked slowly and distinctly.

"Woo Ying has lots of grease in the carriage house. For Aunt M.'s surrey. You could borrow some from Woo Ying."

Still frowning, Father returned his eyes to the piece of bread he was buttering. After a moment he nodded and said, "Aunt Mehitabel's carriage house. Yes, indeed. I'd be very much surprised if there wasn't a bit of axle grease among all those boxes and barrels. Saint Luke must have had Aunt Mehitabel in mind when he spoke of the 'soul that hath much goods laid up for many years.' Charles, you can stop at Greenwood tomorrow and see what Woo Ying can spare."

Father's pale bushy eyebrows had leveled and his voice dropped to its normal range. He nodded again, and from the corners of her eyes Carly could see Nellie and Charles nodding, too, relieved that Father was no longer angry, even if his anger hadn't been directed at them.

Then Father asked Mama how she was feeling and she sighed and said, "A little better," which was what she almost always said, and Father said that was good and began to talk about the apricot crop.

There was going to be a good crop this summer, and with the unusually hot weather the pitting would be under way very soon. The workers' campground was already beginning to fill up, and Father and Arthur had spent most of the morning dealing with the usual problems. The Hooper clan and the Garcías were squabbling already. José and his new wife had set up their tent in a shady spot by the creek that Luther Hooper's brood had staked a claim to, and Luther was threatening to take all his womenfolk up to work at the Hamiltons' pitting shed. Arthur, Father said, had gotten a quick education, this morning, in the problems involved in being shed boss.

"Isn't that right, Arthur?" Father said.

"Yes, sir," Arthur said. "Grammar school, high school, and college, all in one morning." Then in a low voice, under cover of Mama's request for a pillow for her back, he added, "Failed in every subject, I'm afraid."

On her way to the parlor for Mama's back pillow, Carly couldn't help grinning. Arthur was undoubtedly right about being a failure as boss of the pitting shed. She couldn't imagine Arthur successfully keeping track of the boxes pitted by dozens of workers, settling their squabbles, and handling their problems, while Father was busy overseeing the crews in the orchards. But Father had already tried Charles and it had been a disaster. According to Father, every kind of mischief went on under Charles's very nose without his even noticing. Arthur, Carly thought, would notice every bit of mischief—and be right in the middle of it. Carly could just imagine Arthur flirting with one of the pretty Mexican girls like Estrellita García, while the rest of the pitting crew quarreled and loafed and packed up dried apricots to sell to their relatives when they got back home. So there was probably going to be another disaster—and it would be one more thing to blame on Alfred Bennington Quigley.

It was Quigley's fault because he was the one who had made the Hartwicks lose Carmen. For several years, ever since she was fifteen, Nellie, who was a natural-born shed boss, had worked in the pitting shed. But that was when Carmen worked for the Hartwicks, cooking and cleaning and taking care of Mama. Now, however, with money so scarce, Father had let Carmen go, and so Nellie could no longer be spared from her housekeeping duties. So the Hartwicks lacked a shed boss, just as they lacked a telephone and an indoor toilet, and all of it was because of the Quigleys.

The discussion of the pitting-shed problems and the feud between the Hoopers and the Garcías had held Carly's attention, but when she returned to the table with Mama's pillow, Father had begun to talk about politics and what President Roosevelt had said about Cuba. So she stopped listening and began to think about condors, and for a while she almost forgot about being in trouble with Nellie. But when dinner was over and she was helping with the dishes, she found that she was not yet forgiven.

❧❀❧ *chapter 13*

That night, as Carly helped with the after-dinner cleanup, neither Lila nor Nellie spoke to her or even looked in her direction. Ignoring her when she tried to explain or apologize, and even when she tried to tell them about the dead condor by the spring, they hurried through the clearing and washing. Lila finished her chores first and left, pointedly saying good night only to Nellie. Carly was mournfully drying the last of the china, when Nellie hung her apron in the pantry and came back into the kitchen. Pouring herself the last few drops of coffee, she sat down at the kitchen table.

"I don't understand how you can be so thoughtless," she began. "I was really frightened for you, Carly."

"For me? Why were you frightened for me?"

"I was so sure you wouldn't be late tonight, when you knew Father would be here and how angry he'd be."

"I don't know," Carly said. "I guess I just wasn't thinking for a while, about Father being angry, I mean."

Nellie's frown softened to a puzzled look. "You weren't thinking about Father being angry?" she repeated, making it

80

into a question. "How can you not think about . . . ?" She stopped for a moment and her frown returned. "I was frightened because I was so sure you wouldn't be late unless there'd been an accident, or something had happened to you. Charles said you'd gone up into the hills on the Kellys' donkeys, and I just felt sure the donkey had slipped on one of those narrow trails, or something else awful had happened."

"No," Carly said. "Nothing bad happened. I just forgot. It was so exciting—seeing the condor and the other dead one by the spring. I just forgot how late it was."

"And then when I saw that you were all right, and that it was just carelessness again . . ." Nellie paused and then went on, sounding more angry than ever. "Carly, if you don't mind upsetting Father, you should remember that I do. And Charles most of all. Didn't you stop to think that if Father had known what happened he would have blamed Charles because he'd given you permission to go?"

Of course. That explained Charles's anger. "I guess I just didn't think," Carly admitted.

"No." Nellie's voice was bitter. "You don't think. You just don't think about how other people feel. I was so angry when you came in and I saw that nothing had happened and that you had simply disobeyed again. I would have gone straight to Father and told him, if it hadn't been for Charles. Charles was sure that Father would be furious at him for letting you go. Poor Charles was so worried."

"I'm sorry," Carly said. "I'm sorry Charles was so worried." She slowly put away the dishpans and hung up her towel in the pantry. When she came back into the kitchen, Nellie was still sitting at the table holding her coffee cup between her hands. She was looking at Carly, but she didn't look quite as angry. Carly smiled hopefully and sat down across the table.

"Nellie," she said, "what would Father have done to Charles if he'd found out?"

Nellie frowned. "What do you mean?"

"I mean, what if Rosemary really did fall down the cliff with me and I broke my neck—and Charles had told me that I could go. What would Father do to Charles? Would he make him stay in his room for a week, like I had to when I went swimming in the water tank? Or would he disinherit him and make him go out in the world to seek his fortune like in—"

"Oh, Carly!" Nellie thumped the coffee cup down on the table and jumped to her feet. "You are just incorrigible. Making up nonsense like that instead of thinking about how thoughtless you've been and how much trouble you've caused everybody. Of course Father wouldn't have disinherited Charles. And it's not that Charles is afraid of what Father would do to him. It's just that Father does get very upset when people don't do what they should, and Charles hates to upset him."

Carly shook her head. "I don't know," she said. "Are you sure?"

"Am I sure about what?"

"That Charles isn't afraid of Father. It seems to me—"

Nellie's eyes were flashing again and the angry red was spreading on her cheeks. "Now you listen to me, Mehitabel Carlton Hartwick. It's you who should be more afraid. Everyone used to think it was so cute the way you were such a fearless baby, going up to strangers and big dogs, and climbing on everything, and standing up to Father and other grown-ups. But it's not so cute anymore when it causes other people so much grief. You should be afraid to be such a wicked, thoughtless child—afraid that not only your father but God, too, will be angry at you for causing so much trouble. Now you just march right up to your room and say your prayers and ask God to forgive you."

"Nellie, I . . ." Carly began, and then gave up. Sometimes it just seemed impossible to know what would make Nellie angry. "All right," she said. "I'm going."

In her room Carly threw herself down on the bed and stared at the ceiling. They were all angry at her. All but Father and Mama, and the only reason they weren't was because they hadn't even noticed that she was missing. All her family either hated her or didn't care about her at all. She began to breathe deeply and blink her eyes rapidly, and in only a few seconds the tears came. Hot and wet, they spilled up from the corners of her eyes and rolled down her cheeks. After she'd cried for several minutes she rearranged herself on the bed with her head on the pillow and her feet neatly side by side. Then she folded her arms over her chest and clasped an imaginary lily with both hands.

She was dying. Her heart was so broken that it would soon cease to beat, and when they came in she would be cold and stiff, staring lifelessly at the ceiling. They would bury her in the graveyard next to poor little Petey and then people would write sad poetry about her and cry whenever her name was mentioned. And Aunt M. and Woo Ying . . .

Thinking about how Aunt M. and Woo Ying would respond to the news of her sudden death was sad—but somehow comforting. Thinking of the two of them beside her lonely grave reminded her of the grave Woo Ying had helped her make for her pet canary—how they had made little gifts of paper and burned them, so that the smoke would carry the gifts up to heaven, as people did in China when somebody died. Her cheeks were almost dry and she was beginning to feel sleepy, when there was a tap on the door and Nellie came in.

Standing beside the bed, Nellie looked down at Carly, her

face expressionless. Carly stared back, wide awake now, and wondering.

"What are you doing?" Nellie said. "Why aren't you ready for bed?"

"I was thinking," Carly said.

"Have you said your prayers?"

"No," Carly said. "Not exactly."

Nellie shook her head reprovingly, but then the corners of her mouth curled up in a reluctant smile. She held out her hand. "Jump up now. I'll unbutton your dress while I'm here."

Carly jumped up and turned her back and quick fingers began to work their way down her spine. The fingers were firm and quick, but their gentleness plainly said that Nellie was no longer angry. Carly felt a rush of relief, followed a moment later by an uneasy feeling that she didn't really deserve to be forgiven. It was true that she hadn't even thought about poor Charles being blamed. And what if Nellie knew that she'd only been playing dead and feeling sorry for herself when she should have been repenting and asking God for forgiveness? Guilt descended, a heavy weight on her shoulders and a bitter taste in her mouth. She took a long, shuddering breath.

"Oh, Nellie. It seems like it's so hard for me to remember to be good. I don't see why I couldn't be just naturally good, like you."

Nellie took Carly by the shoulders and turned her around. She was smiling in a strange, unhappy way. "Oh, Carly," she said. "That's such a foolish thing to say. Sometimes I think there's nothing very natural about any of us." She pulled Carly closer and gave her a quick kiss on top of the head, and added, "Except perhaps for you."

"What do you mean?" Carly asked quickly, but Nellie only shook her head and hurried out of the room. Carly sighed deeply. It was so frustrating when Nellie said things like that and then wouldn't explain what she meant.

Like the time Carly had offered to stay with Mama while Nellie and Lila went shopping and Mama had said Carly was too irresponsible because she'd been spoiled by living at Greenwood for so long. And afterward in the kitchen Nellie had slammed things around and said, "Spoiled! She should talk about people being spoiled!" But when Carly asked if she meant that Mama was spoiled, too, Nellie had only frowned and said what she always did—that Anna and Ezra Hartwick were the best parents anyone could ask for, "—and don't you ever forget it, Carly Hartwick."

Carly sighed again, crawled into bed, and stopped worrying by thinking, instead, about condors.

❧✳❀ *chapter 14*

By Sunday the unseasonable hot spell had ended and the usual weather pattern for May and June—foggy mornings and cool, sunny afternoons—had returned. Getting ready for church, Carly decided that it was cold enough to wear her new coat. Not new exactly, but a recent hand-me-down from Lila, it was a lovely shade of periwinkle-blue and had a wide sash belt. Nellie had taken up the hem, but it was still a bit longer than most of the things in Carly's closet. The new longer length made her feel older, almost grown-up. And something, perhaps the fact that the coat had looked so beautiful on Lila, made Carly feel beautiful too. She was ready to go, shoes buttoned and coat belted, when Nellie came in to help with her hair bow.

"All ready," Nellie said. "Good." Then she sighed. "All except your hair."

"I brushed it," Carly protested. "It just won't lie flat. And that new ribbon just won't make a bow. See. I tried and tried and it just looks like a wad."

"Let me see what I can do," Nellie said.

She untied the wadded ribbon and loosened Carly's troublesome hair, thick and brown and just curly enough to be unruly. After brushing it firmly, she pulled it back, tied it with a bit of string, and then with the stubborn new ribbon. Carly watched in the mirror as Nellie skillfully coaxed the white satin folds into a bow so wide that it stood out like wings on each side of her head.

"There," Nellie said. "You look lovely. Hurry downstairs now. Charles has the surrey out front. And don't forget to say good-bye to Father and Mama."

In the parlor Father was seated next to Mama's sofa. Carly stopped for a moment in the doorway to admire them. On Sundays Father always wore a tie and his gray suit. Mama was wearing her best Chelsea cloth wrapper with her new white shawl over her shoulders. They looked, Carly always thought, like Robert Browning, the famous poet, and his beautiful invalid wife, Elizabeth.

On the lamp table beside Father's chair were the big family Bible, *Harrison's Anthology of Notable Sermons,* and Ralph Waldo Emerson's *Conduct of Life.* Every Sunday, while the rest of the family went to church, Father stayed at home and read to Mama. It was a sacrifice that he made so the rest of the family could attend church regularly. That was what he'd said to Reverend Mapes one day when the preacher was visiting. Afterward, while Father was walking the preacher out to his buggy, Arthur said it was a sacrifice he'd be only too glad to make, if Father would only let him.

"Maybe he'd let you," Carly said. "Why don't you ask him?"

"Not a chance," Arthur said. "If he ever lets anyone miss church, it won't be a rascal like me. Or you either." He grabbed Carly and tickled her. "Or you, either, you little sinner."

She had giggled when Arthur tickled her, but afterward

she wondered about sins in general and hers and Arthur's in particular. She had a feeling that Arthur's were a great deal more exciting than her own, but when she asked him about them he only laughed.

She was still standing in the doorway thinking about sin and sacrifice when Father looked up from his book and saw her. "Carly," he said, "what are you doing there? I think the others are all ready."

"Ah"—Mama turned her head on the curved headrest of the sofa—"you're wearing Lila's coat. It looks quite nice on you." She held out her hand. "I do hope you've remembered to clean your nails."

"Yes, I did." Carly put her hands in Mama's and left them there. Mama's hands were incredibly soft. When she had looked at Carly's nails she took her hands away and put them back under the edge of her shawl.

"And what verses have you prepared?" Father asked.

"We only had to learn one for today," Carly said. "There's going to be a visiting preacher, and Mrs. Mapes said it would be nice if we all learned the text for his sermon. The text is"—Carly stood up straight with her hands gracefully clasped, as she had learned in Mrs. Reed's elocution class—"Matthew twenty-three, thirty-three. 'Ye serpents, ye generation of vipers, how can you escape the damnation of hell?' "

"Oh, dear," Mama said.

"Yes, I see," Father said. "It seems that Santa Luisa's sinners are to be dangled over the fiery pit again. Ah, well, there are certainly those who might benefit by a slight scorching. Run along now, Carly. As usual, you've kept everyone waiting."

Carly would have liked to ask a question, or perhaps two. She would have liked to know who needed scorching and also why, but when Father said run along, you ran.

In the surrey Lila and Nellie were in back under the

fringed sunshade, but Carly chose to squeeze in between her brothers on the driver's seat. Arthur flipped the reins across old Prince's back, and they started off at a fast trot.

The ride into Santa Luisa went very quickly. Carly told Arthur some of the things she'd learned from Matt about condors, and Arthur said what did Matt know about it? So she explained how Matt had learned all about condors from his grandfather. Arthur laughed and said, "What does that uneducated old squatter know?" But Nellie said Dan Kelly probably knew a lot. Nellie said that, according to Mr. Wolfson, the high school principal, Dan Kelly was a self-taught authority on the wildlife of Ventura County. "Don't you remember hearing Mr. Wolfson say that?" she asked Lila. But Lila only shrugged and said that condors were disgusting and that she was sure that they were terribly dangerous, just like Arthur said.

After that Carly told about the ruined sign and the dead condor at the spring, and how Matt said it was Henry and Bucky who had done it, and everyone began to talk at once. Arthur said that if he caught Henry Babcock on Carlton property, whether he was shooting condors or whatever, he'd pick him up and shake the pants off him, and Nellie told Arthur not to be vulgar. Charles was asking Carly to explain again how Matt had known it was Henry who'd shot the condor, when Lila sighed so loudly that everyone turned to look at her. She was looking disgusted again. Carly was sure that Lila was the only person in the world who could look disgusted so beautifully. Curling her delicate upper lip, she wrinkled her short, straight nose and asked why they had to talk about revolting things like condors and Quigleys on Sunday morning.

Carly was agreeing that she felt the same way about the Quigleys, particularly Henry, when suddenly there they were in front of Greenwood. Aunt Mehitabel's chestnut mare,

Chloe, was tied to the hitching post and Woo Ying was waiting by the surrey with the step stool. In a flash Carly climbed over Arthur and jumped. She landed with a thud, her skirts flying, and Prince shied and skittered sideways. As Carly climbed up into the surrey she could still hear Nellie scolding and Arthur laughing as he pulled Prince around and the surrey started off down the road.

Carly always rode the rest of the way to church with Aunt M. and Woo Ying. Usually she sat up front with Woo Ying and leaned back over the seat so Aunt M. could hear, too, and told them all the news from the ranch house. Today there was more news than usual, all about the condors, and how it looked like Henry Babcock and his friend Bucky Hansen had been hanging around Carlton Spring shooting them.

Aunt M. and Woo Ying were a much better audience than her brothers and sisters had been. Except for amazed exclamations they listened in silence, and Aunt M. was still muttering and shaking her head and Woo Ying was still saying "Aiii" under his breath when the surrey pulled up in front of the church.

✺✺✺ *chapter 15*

The Presbyterian church in Santa Luisa was a fine stone building with a tall central spire, and wide front steps. On the steps
and the pathway that led to it, Santa Luisa's Presbyterians
were now slowly making their way into the building, or stopping to chat with other recent arrivals.

As Woo Ying tied Chloe to the hitching rail beside Prince,
Carly noticed Arthur, Charles, and Lila going up the steps
and disappearing inside the church. Nellie didn't seem to be
with them, and Carly guessed "Clarence" before she even
saw them. She looked around quickly and sure enough, there
was Nellie talking to gawky old Clarence Buford, near the
pine tree on the church lawn. Clarence, who had what Aunt
M. called unfortunate teeth, and a funny loose-jointed way of
walking, had followed Nellie around ever since grammar
school. Arthur said that Clarence would have come courting
Nellie long ago, if he weren't so afraid of Father, and Lila
said that Nellie shouldn't be so nice to impossible people like
Clarence, because it only encouraged them.

91

"Come on, missy," Woo Ying said. "Don't make Auntie wait."

Carly stopped staring at Nellie and Clarence and jumped down, ignoring Woo Ying's step stool. But after she caught up with Aunt M., she turned to wave and smile. Woo Ying would put on Chloe's feed bag and then stay there by the surrey until everyone else had gone into the church before he came in to sit in the last pew near the door. She turned to wave again as she went up the steps with Aunt M.

The row reserved for Mrs. Mapes's Intermediates was unusually crowded. Squeezing in between Mavis Johns and Edith Jenkins, Carly stuck her elbow in Edith's ribs and whispered, "Scoot," but Edith didn't. Instead she only rolled her eyes and sat still. "Look," she whispered. Carly looked and there, only a foot away from Edith—the foot that Edith wouldn't scoot—was Henry Babcock.

Carly was surprised, because although Henry Babcock was a Presbyterian like the rest of the Quigleys, and a nominal member of the Intermediate Sunday School class, he was hardly ever there. Henry's parents and grandfather only came to the eleven o'clock service, so Henry was sent to Sunday School all by himself every Sunday morning at a quarter to ten—and almost never arrived until eleven o'clock.

According to rumor Henry usually spent the Sunday School hour fooling around with some older boys—scallywags, mostly, whose families lived down by the river, and who never went to Sunday School or church either. And some people said he'd been one of the gang of rascals who'd dropped a live rat through the window of the Catholic Church during ten o'clock mass.

Nobody could imagine how Henry got away with ditching Sunday School, because the Quigley-Babcocks had certainly heard about Henry's bad attendance record from Mrs.

Mapes. Not to mention a lot of other transgressions they must have heard about from some other people, including some very angry Catholics. But what most people believed was that Henry never got punished because his grandfather, old Alfred Bennington Quigley, wouldn't hear of it.

Everybody said that no man alive had ever doted on a child as much as old Mr. Quigley doted on Henry. He'd never had a son, and when his only child, Alicia, married he couldn't wait to have a whole lot of wonderful grandsons. But all the poor man ever got was Henry. And what Henry got was spoiled, within an inch of his life.

After the first moment of surprise Carly remembered the ruined sign and the poor dead condor and her surprise turned to anger. She glared at Henry until he turned to look at her, and then went on glaring for several seconds, squinting her eyes and trying to look daggers. For a moment Henry's flat brown eyes stared back, as blank and shiny as two marbles, but then he wrinkled up his pug nose and stuck out his tongue. Carly tossed her head and looked away.

After the greeting by Reverend Mapes there were two hymns and a prayer and then the visiting minister was introduced. His name was Brother Tupper and he had, he said, been called by God to come all the way from North Carolina to preach to sinners in California. Brother Tupper was a short, roundish man with a red face and a soft southern accent, and his words slurred together in an interesting way as he said how glad he was to see such a fine large congregation, and how he hoped that everyone, and especially the children, would stay after Sunday School to hear the word of God. Then they all marched to their classes while Miss Higginbotham played "Onward Christian Soldiers" on the piano.

On the church steps Carly stopped and told Mavis to go on and save her a chair, and when the boys went by she called to Henry.

"What do you want, Mehitabel?" Henry said, but he stopped and the other boys went on without him, snickering and making smarty remarks about Henry having a girlfriend.

Carly glared at Henry and he stepped back—outside of kicking range. She'd kicked him in the shins once when he threw a stone at Tiger. "What's eating you now?" he asked uneasily.

"I just wanted to tell you," Carly said, "that I know who was trespassing on Carlton property, and who shot that poor condor and hung it over our sign. And—and"—Carly took a deep breath—"and if you ever do anything like that again, you're going to be very very sorry."

Henry's naturally blank face had gone even blanker. "How'd you know—" he started, before he caught himself and said, "What are you talking about, Hartwick? I don't know anything about any condor."

"Yes, you do," Carly said. "The whole matter is under investigation and you are going to be in serious trouble."

But Henry's open-mouthed stare had turned into his usual spiteful grin. "What trouble?" he said. "I can shoot condors anytime I want to, and as far as that spring goes, it's as much Quigley property as Carlton, and my Grandpa is going to prove it."

"No, it's not," Carly said. "It isn't either."

"No, it's not. It isn't either," Henry said in a mocking falsetto voice, and then he laughed and ran off after the other boys.

The Intermediate class met in the dining room of the parsonage so Mrs. Mapes could teach the class in between trips to the kitchen to see how her Sunday dinner was doing. As soon as everyone had found a chair, including some that had to be brought in from the kitchen, Mrs. Mapes said how pleased she was to see so many scholars in attendance on this fine Sunday morning. And the next thing she said was that it was a good thing so many were present, because on this very day someone would be chosen to represent the Intermediate class on the church float in the Fourth of July parade. The float was to be pulled by Mr. Quigley's beautiful dapple-grays, and it would be decorated with flowers and crepe paper, and everyone on it would wear costumes representing themes of a patriotic nature.

Carly caught her breath, and forgot all about Henry and the condor and everything but the Fourth of July parade. Just last year Lila had been the Statue of Liberty on the high school float and she had looked so wonderful with her dark hair loose and hanging down over her white robe. People had talked for days and days about what a beautiful statue Lila had been. Picturing herself in Lila's white robe and spiky golden crown, Carly felt a sudden pang of yearning. There was nothing in the whole world that she wanted more than to be the Statue of Liberty on the Presbyterian Fourth of July float.

Looking around the room, Carly assessed her chances of being chosen and decided they were pretty good. Of course, she wasn't as beautiful as Lila, but she'd had good luck in winning elections in the past. She'd been elected class president once, and Queen of the May twice, and secretary so many times she'd lost track. Being elected secretary might not mean a great deal, since it depended mostly on spelling ability, but presidents and Queens of the May were chosen for more complicated reasons. Carly wasn't entirely sure just what those reasons were, but she did know that she often did well in elections. She was thinking that her chances were pretty good—until she noticed what Henry was up to.

While Mrs. Mapes took up the collection and counted it, and filled out the register, Henry whispered to Luther Purdy and Emma Hawkins and then reached in his pocket and gave them something. She was beginning to suspect the truth, even before Mavis Johns told her what was going on. When Mrs. Mapes went into the kitchen to check on her pork roast, Mavis moved closer to Carly and whispered that Henry was buying votes for the float election. His mother, Alicia Babcock, was on the float committee and she'd told him that each Sunday School class would get to choose one participant. And Henry had been rounding up votes ever since.

"He already got Bucky and Frank," Mavis whispered excitedly, "and I think he just got Luther and Emma."

"How about you?" Carly whispered. "Are you going to vote for him?"

Mavis smiled sheepishly. "I'd rather vote for you, Carly," she said. "You know that." She reached in her pocket and pulled out a shiny new dime. She looked at the dime and then at Carly. "You don't have an extra dime, do you?" she asked. "I'll give Henry's back if you do."

Mrs. Mapes came back then, so all Carly could do was toss her head and turn her back on Mavis, and think about the remarks she could have made about people who sold their friendship.

The lesson started then. The assignment had been to read all of Matthew 23 as well as memorizing verse 33, and the quiz was about everything in the whole chapter. The questions weren't easy, but Carly had read Matthew 23 just that morning before breakfast, so it was fresh in her mind. Henry made a mess of most of his answers, but, as usual, he managed to make a joke out of his mistakes, so that the class had a good time laughing at him. When Mr$. Mapes asked him what building was described as being "white and clean on the outside and full of uncleanness on the inside," he said, "a whitewashed outhouse," and everyone nearly died laughing. And when Carly gave the right answer, which was, of course, a whited sepulcher, Henry whispered, "Know-it-all! Just like her pa."

When the clock on the dining room wall said ten fifty-five, Henry raised his hand and asked when the election was going to be, and that's when Mrs. Mapes said that there wasn't going to be one. "I decided I would select as our representative the person with the most correct answers to today's quiz," she said, "and the honor goes, without question, to Carly Hartwick." Carly marched back into the church in such a haze of excitement that she barely noticed how everyone was avoiding Henry, in case he decided to demand the return of his dimes.

chapter 16

Carly had been looking forward to Brother Tupper's "generation of vipers" sermon because she felt quite certain it was going to be about sin. The Reverend Mapes was always disappointingly vague on the subject of sins and sinners, but there had been some visiting preachers in the past who had dropped some fascinating hints. Carly had been hoping that Brother Tupper would do the same.

It wasn't at all hard, of course, to get information about the ordinary, everyday sins. But it was obvious that God wouldn't have gone to all the trouble to create hell just to pay people back for things like disobedience and immodesty. So it was pretty certain there were a lot of much more interesting sins that no one would talk about, at least not to Carly. And right at first Brother Tupper's sermon seemed promising.

Brother Tupper began by talking in his soft southern voice about how the world was becoming more evil and sinful all the time, and most of it was because of atheists. The atheists, he said, were spreading all over the country like a plague.

According to Brother Tupper a lot of terrible things were going on in the world, things like immoral books and stage shows and strikes and bombings and assassinations, and the atheists were behind them all. Brother Tupper worked himself up to a rasping red-faced bellow over the atheists, and Carly was looking forward to what else he was going to say about sin when he suddenly changed the subject. After that he only talked about the End of the World.

The End of the World was coming very soon. Brother Tupper was sure of it, and he read a lot of verses from the Bible to prove it. The verses told about signs that would come just before the world ended—and all the signs had happened already or were just about to happen. Just before the end there would be wars and rumors of wars, and famines and earthquakes, and, the most convincing of all, horseless carriages. Brother Tupper reminded everyone about the wars in Casablanca and Moldavia, and the famine in China, and nobody needed to be reminded about the San Francisco earthquake, or horseless carriages like the one the Quigleys had just bought. There didn't seem to be any doubt about it—the last days were well under way.

After church that day Carly went home with Aunt M. and Woo Ying, as she always did on Sunday afternoons, and all the way to Greenwood she was still thinking about the sermon and the end of the world. She didn't even mention about being chosen to ride on the Fourth of July float, since it seemed pretty certain that the world wasn't going to last that long.

Woo Ying started talking about what they were going to have for Sunday dinner, which was ordinarily a subject that Carly found interesting after the long morning in church. But with the world about to end, even chicken and dumplings and strawberry pie seemed unimportant. But it wasn't until Aunt M. and Carly got out at the front gate, and Woo Ying had taken Chloe and the surrey on to the stable, that Aunt M. said, "Carly, child, what is the matter? You don't seem like yourself at all."

At first Carly shook her head because she was afraid what she wanted to ask would sound awfully selfish, but by the time they got to the veranda she couldn't stand it any longer. "Aunt M.," she said, "do you think the world will end before the Fourth of July parade?—because I was going to get to be the Statue of Liberty on the Presbyterian float."

Aunt M. blew up. "Ridiculous!" she shouted, stomping down the hall, dragging Carly after her by the arm. "That ridiculous, sanctimonious old hayseed," she yelled, shoving Carly down into a chair by the kitchen table. Stomping over to the sink, she began to pump water into the tea kettle, still shouting. "Red-faced—self-righteous—heartless old pulpit-thumper. Going around the country showing off his piety by scaring little children to death." She was still shouting when Woo Ying came in the back door.

"Stop that," Woo Ying hollered. "Be sick again, yell like that!" He took the tea kettle away from Aunt M. and made her sit down at the kitchen table and got her nerve medicine out of the cupboard.

Aunt M. sat down quietly enough, but after a moment she got her breath back and began to yell at Woo Ying. "I don't need that. There's nothing wrong with my nerves. And don't you tell me what to do, you ridiculous—"

But Woo Ying was yelling, too, drowning her out. "Why yelling like that at poor missy? Look how sad missy. Look at poor little missy Carly."

Aunt M. stopped yelling and looked at Carly and so did Woo Ying. She looked back at them. They were both peering at her with their wrinkled faces squeezed into worried frowns. Suddenly she began to giggle, and after a moment

Aunt M. laughed too. But Woo Ying went on frowning until Aunt M. explained.

"I wasn't yelling at Carly," she said. "I was yelling about that caterwauling, puddin'-mouthed old preacher. Scared Carly half to death with all his talk about the world coming to an end." She turned to Carly. "Listen to me, child. The world's not going to come to an end. Not now and not for a long time. That—that"—she muttered a few more words under her breath and then went on—"that Brother Tupper doesn't know what he's talking about."

Carly nodded. She wanted to believe what Aunt M. said. She didn't want to think about all those terribly convincing signs and omens the preacher had shouted about. She wished she could just forget all those proofs that the end was at hand.

Woo Ying was nodding his head. "Aha," he said. "Woo Ying think maybe reason why missy so sad. Woo Ying think maybe missy worry about end of world." He sat down in the chair next to Carly and tucked his hands into his sleeves. "Look at Woo Ying," he said. "Woo Ying very old. In China very old people very wise. Know many things. Woo Ying know all about world. World very okay. Very okay." He leaned forward and stared into Carly's eyes. "Missy believe Woo Ying?"

Carly felt a smile tugging at the edges of her mouth. "Yes," she said. "I believe Woo Ying."

chapter 17

"For heaven's sake, Carly, stand still."

"I am standing still," Carly said. "I'm not moving anything but my eyes."

Perched on a footstool in front of the long mirror in Nellie's room, Carly turned her head ever so slightly and rolled her eyes toward her reflection. The crown looked fine again, now that Nellie had pressed the wrinkled points with the flatiron, and the torch with its flames of orange and yellow tissue paper was as good as new. The gown itself was another matter.

Silky white and draped in Grecian fashion, the Statue of Liberty gown that had been so stunning on Lila was something of a disappointment. The bodice, a crisscrossing of softly gathered tucks, had fitted quite differently on Lila. Carly sighed. Taking a deep breath, she lifted her chest as much as she could, without much effect.

"Nellie," she asked, "when will I grow a bosom?"

Nellie started, as if she had pricked her finger. "Ummm," she said, shaking her head and pointing to the pins she was holding between her lips. Then she bent her head quickly again over the hemming, but not quickly enough to hide the frown. Looking down at her sister's curly red head, Carly sighed again, more softly. The question about bosoms, like lots of other questions, was one that Nellie probably wouldn't answer, even if she hadn't had a mouth full of pins.

Carly had learned by experience that Nellie disliked being asked certain kinds of questions almost as much as she disliked being "in charge." "Ask your mother," she usually said when Carly asked about such things. Carly guessed that Nellie had read somewhere that "Ask your mother" was what you were supposed to say to children who were too curious. But whoever had given that advice obviously hadn't known Mama.

Not that Mama refused to answer such questions. It was just that the answer never had much to do with what you had asked. Usually what Mama had to say turned into a long story about how little she had known or even guessed about the troubles and burdens of life when she was a child—in the state of Maine. And about how innocent and carefree and happy the little Anna Elliot, the beloved daughter of Joshua and Eliza Elliot, had been in those long ago days. When she was finally finished you didn't have any answers except for a vague feeling that not knowing anything way back then, in the state of Maine, was a lot more fun than not knowing anything in California in 1907.

Having given up on the question about bosoms, it occurred to Carly to wonder about Nellie's plans for the Fourth.

"Nellie," she asked, "who's going to stay home with Mama on the Fourth? Is Father?"

Nellie shook her head. Taking the remaining pins out of her mouth, she sat back on her heels and looked critically at the pinned-up hem. "Turn around slowly," she said.

103

"Is he? He is, isn't he?" Carly repeated as she turned, her arms outstretched. She was beginning to worry. Although Father disliked parades and picnics and all such "entertainments," he now and then decided that it was necessary for him to attend. "Not that I'd prefer to," Carly had heard him say. "A matter of diplomacy. Can't have our good neighbors thinking that I'm bored by their rustic social efforts."

Carly wasn't worried for herself—she wouldn't be the one to stay home. If there had been times in the past when she felt hurt that Mama considered her too irresponsible, this wasn't one of them. She would hate having to stay home on the Fourth, and she was sure Nellie would too.

Nellie shook her head slowly. "He's not going to the parade. But he says that Aunt M. thinks he should go to the picnic to talk to people and find out what's being said about the water company. Aunt M. wants him to see if he can find out if enough people want the city to challenge Mr. Quigley's control. She thinks we'll need—"

"Oh, Nellie!" Carly interrupted. "Will you have to stay home?"

"I'm to go to the parade. But I'll have to come home before the picnic starts." Nellie shrugged, smiling ruefully. "And just when Clarence got up his nerve to ask me to sit with him at the picnic."

Carly stared at Nellie, suddenly seeing her in an entirely new light. "Did he? Really, Nellie? Did you say yes?" Although Clarence had been around for a long time, talking to Nellie when there was an opportunity, blushing madly and smiling his toothy smile, it had never occurred to Carly to think of him and Nellie in romantic terms. One naturally thought of Lila that way—Lila and her Johnny and scenes from forbidden, doomed romances like *Romeo and Juliet* and *Wuthering Heights* and *Lorna Doone*. But when one thought of Nellie the things that came to mind first were worried frowns and lectures. And then, of course, those sudden hugs and kisses—and cookies—and hems taken up and wrinkled crowns straightened.

Feeling guilty, Carly poked Nellie's shoulder and asked again in her most enthusiastic tone of voice, "Did you tell him you would? That's so exciting. I think that's very exciting." She wasn't just pretending either. After all, there was no doubt that sitting with a young man at the Fourth of July picnic instead of with your family was a fairly romantic event —even if the man was only Clarence Buford.

Nellie's smile was teasing but also, somehow, sad. "I was still deciding," she said. "And now I don't have to. Perhaps it's all for the best."

On the night before the Fourth, Carly had trouble sleeping. She tossed and turned until her nightgown was wrapped around her body like swaddling clothes and she had to stand up in bed to straighten herself out. Then she got back under the covers and tossed and turned some more. At last she got up and went downstairs for Tiger.

Strictly speaking, Tiger wasn't allowed in the house because Mama was an Elliot. The Elliots, Mama's family back in Maine, didn't approve of having animals in the house and Mama still felt the same way. So Carly only let Tiger in when she really needed him—and when nobody was looking. But ever since she first got Tiger, right after she'd come to live at the ranch house, she sometimes needed him to help her sleep. Nobody else knew about it. It was her secret, and Tiger's.

Tiger knew it was a secret. No matter how quietly she opened the back door he always heard, and he'd be at the door in a second, wagging his tail like crazy but not making a sound. She'd pick him up then, because his toenails on the stairs were too noisy, and tiptoe upstairs. Usually Tiger yipped when he was excited, but he never did on the way to

Carly's room, even though he was absolutely vibrating with happiness and excitement. Instead he only made a tiny growling sound almost like a cat purring and licked Carly's cheek or ear or whatever else he could reach. Back in her room, with Tiger cuddled up beside her on top of the blankets, she usually went right to sleep and didn't wake up until it was time to tiptoe him back downstairs before Nellie went down to the kitchen.

It worked again that night. With Tiger beside her Carly slept peacefully until dawn, when she got up to let him out—and to start preparing to be the Statue of Liberty. In spite of having to wash her hair to get out the braid crinkles, Carly was, for once, the one who was ready on time. Robed and crowned and with her slightly damp hair hanging loose on her shoulders, she fretted nervously while her brothers took forever to eat and dress, and Lila and Nellie fussed endlessly over the food they were taking to the picnic. By the time Arthur brought the surrey to the front steps, and Charles, in his slow, uncertain way, loaded and shifted and reloaded the baskets of picnic supplies, Carly was almost beside herself.

All the way into town behind poky old Prince, she worried and fussed, certain that the parade would be under way by the time they arrived, and she would have missed forever her opportunity to be a patriotic symbol. But although it was already five minutes past nine when Arthur finally reined to a stop at the assembly area near the end of First Street, the milling mob had only begun to form itself into a marching column.

"They're still there," Carly squealed, bouncing in excitement. "They didn't leave without me, after all."

❧❀❧ *chapter 18*

The moment the surrey stopped, Carly leapt to the ground, Grecian robe flying. Behind her she could hear Nellie scolding and Arthur and Charles laughing as she straightened her crown and started off at a run around a team of bays hitched to a buckboard decorated with red, white, and blue streamers.

Near the buckboard a group of Women's Club ladies, dressed in colonial costumes, waited as Mr. Hamilton and his grown-up son, Sam, struggled to get Mrs. Hamilton up onto the wagon bed. Mrs. Clara Hamilton, who was president of the Women's Club, was wearing across her broad bosom a red ribbon with BETSY ROSS printed on it. On the wagon a copy of the original American flag was draped over a quilting frame, and around it the club ladies would represent Betsy Ross and her sewing circle, stitching up the famous first flag.

Ducking around Betsy Ross and her friends, Carly found herself in the midst of the Community Marching Band. In red and white uniforms decorated with lots of gold braid, the men and boys of the band were forming ranks and warming up their instruments. Carly dodged between tootling cornets and throbbing tubas and, a few yards beyond the band, finally arrived at the Presbyterian Church's entry—the "Symbols of Patriotism."

The Presbyterian float was an enormous freight wagon pulled by the Quigleys' famous matched team, a pair of high-stepping dapple-grays, so light as to be almost white. When Carly arrived, all the other Symbols of Patriotism were already arranged around the bed of the wagon amid huge potted ferns and a number of small latticework trellises covered with real roses. Carly thought she had never seen anything so beautiful in her whole life.

"There she is. Our little Miss Liberty has arrived." Reverend Mapes's loud preacher's voice boomed out from somewhere among the trellises. At least it sounded like Reverend Mapes, but when he leaned down over the driver's seat, holding out his hand, for just a moment she wasn't sure. Looking up against the bright sunlight, she hardly recognized the man in the bushy white wig, three-cornered hat, enormous frock coat, and unnaturally jovial smile. But once up on the wagon bed she saw that it was indeed the preacher, amazingly transformed by his elaborate costume.

Having never seen a preacher's legs before, Carly was looking with interest at the Reverend Mapes's hefty calves encased in tight white stockings, when he suddenly roared again, this time right in her ear.

"Welcome, Miss Liberty, to our illustrious ranks. Captain John Smith here, and may I introduce the lovely Princess Pocahontas." A little guiltily Carly shifted her gaze from the fat white legs to the sweeping gesture that indicated Mrs. Mapes, who was wearing long braids of black yarn and an Indian maiden's dress made from quite a lot of embroidered gunny sacks.

Carly curtsied to the Princess and then followed the Captain between trellises and potted ferns as he introduced her to the other lucky Symbols of Patriotism. The winners from the other Sunday School competitions were sixteen-year-old Ralph Bodger from the young people's class as George Washington, Tommy Fenner from the infants' class as a very small and roly-poly Uncle Sam, and George Freebody, representing the adult class, who was supposed to be the president himself, Mr. Theodore Roosevelt, dressed for safari in a hunting jacket and Panama hat. Nobody scolded Carly for being late and everyone, except for little Tommy, said hello and told her she made a lovely Statue of Liberty, and even Tommy stopped scratching under his Uncle Sam beard long enough to wave his fingers and grin.

By the time Reverend Mapes had assigned everyone a background trellis and found a box for Uncle Sam to stand on so he could be seen over the potted ferns, Betsy Ross and her ladies had moved into the line of march, the band had formed ranks and begun to play, and the parade was under way.

Framed in her rose-covered trellis, Carly braced herself against the jolting of the wagon and shivered with excitement. Just ahead of her in the driver's seat a lanky, sharp-faced man who worked for the Quigleys tightened the reins and shouted at the dapple-grays. "Easy there. Easy now," he shouted, as the spirited horses, spooked by the noise of the band, tossed their heads and plunged against their collars.

The blare and beat of the band, the high-stepping grace of the dapple-grays, the lurching roll of the wagon as it went over the bumpy ground of the vacant lot and down into the street, and the sight of the long, glittering procession stretching out up First Street turned Carly's shiver into a permanent tremble that quivered up and down her legs and out her arms to the tips of her fingers.

The shiver was unexpected, and unexpectedly exciting. *I'm*

trembling, she thought. *I must be terrified. I don't think I've ever been so terrified before.* It was an interesting idea. Concentrating on being terrified on the inside but calm on the outside, she raised her tissue-paper torch and smiled a bravely dignified smile at the first group of parade watchers on the corner of First and Palm.

That first burst of terror had smoothed itself down into a pleasant tingling excitement by the corner of Second Street, where, amid small clumps of waving spectators, Carly spotted Aunt M. and Woo Ying. Aunt M.'s face, under her broad-brimmed hat, was a wreath of smiles and even Woo Ying, whose public face was always solemnly calm, was grinning broadly. Overcome by delight, Carly forgot to be statuelike and jumped up and down, waving her torch wildly.

The wagon rolled on and Carly lost sight of Aunt M. and Woo Ying. Up ahead, in front of the Olympic Hotel, a solid mass of humanity waited, waving and cheering. Quivering with excitement, Carly regained her dignity and posed herself carefully with her torch held high. Then, just as the Quigley grays pranced grandly into the Main Street turn, a string of powerful firecrackers exploded almost under their hooves. As the deafening explosions echoed and reechoed, the terrified horses reared and then plunged forward in a headlong run. And the Presbyterian float turned into a lurching, tumbling, screaming madhouse.

✿✿✿ *chapter 19*

At the first wild forward plunge of the runaway float Carly's rose trellis tipped over on top of her, pinning her to the bed of the wagon. A moment later little Tommy Fenner flew off the box he'd been standing on and landed across her legs, where he stuck like a leech, clinging to her ankles and screaming his head off. It wasn't at all comfortable, bouncing around on the rough wagon bed under Tommy and the trellis, but it all happened so quickly that Carly's astonishment was just beginning to turn into fear when it was over. The wagon lurched violently one last time and came to a sudden stop. Feeling dazed and hurting a little from splinters and rose thorns, Carly detached Tommy and crawled out from under the trellis and looked around her.

People were running toward the wagon from all directions. Voices were shouting, Tommy was still screaming, and the Quigley grays were snorting and stomping as three or four men clung tightly to their bridles. As she began to get her bearings, Carly could see that the wagon had traveled two blocks down Main Street while she was under the trellis. And during that time a great deal had happened.

The Community Band, which had been in the middle of "The Washington Post March" when the team bolted, had managed to scramble out of the way. Except for a lot of torn and scattered sheet music and one badly trampled trombone, there were no serious casualties in the band.

The Betsy Ross float had come off pretty well too. Afterward Sammy Hamilton, the driver, was hailed as a hero. He had, as he told everyone forever afterward, looked back quickly when he heard the firecrackers, immediately saw what was going to happen, and by reacting instantly was able to get his team to the side of the street in time to avoid the runaway Presbyterians and what might have been a terrible collision.

It was a good thing there was no collision, because even without one, what happened on the church float was bad enough. Reverend Mapes, trying to support his wife, lost his balance and fell, pulling her over on top of him. A very large potted fern rolled over George Freebody's foot, and Ralph Bodger jumped or fell out of the wagon, taking a fern and two trellises with him.

But the worst part was that the parade was over—at least for the Presbyterians. Carly didn't think it was fair, or necessary. She herself was fine, except for a crushed torch and a slightly bent crown, not to mention—and she carefully didn't —a few slivers and thorn pricks. And no one could find anything wrong with Tommy, either, once they got him to stop screaming. So the float still had a Statue of Liberty and an Uncle Sam. But President Roosevelt had some smashed toes and John Smith had a badly wrenched back, and worst of all, George Washington had sprained his ankle when he jumped overboard. So the float was taken out of the parade and Carly was heartbroken—at least for a while.

For those first few minutes she could think only that her wonderful day was over and done with, but before long she realized that she was now not only the Statue of Liberty but also a heroine. By the time the parade was finally under way again, the story of what had happened was all over Santa Luisa, and everyone, even people who had not been present at the corner of Palm and Main, knew what had happened. Carly had hardly given up on the float and started to walk down Main Street when she was surrounded by dozens of excited people who wanted to hug and pat her and even cry a little as they praised God for having spared her life. The main parade might have gone on without her, but Carly in her torn and rumpled robe and lopsided crown had become the center of a small personal parade by the time she found the rest of her family.

She'd gotten as far as the fire station before her sisters and brothers came running up the street. Nellie was in tears and even Lila might almost have been. It was hard to tell with Lila, whose face never wrinkled up and got ugly when she cried, as other people's did. Charles was flushed and stammering and Arthur kept saying just wait until he got his hands on the murderer who'd thrown those firecrackers. Then Aunt M. arrived with Woo Ying, and before they had finished fussing, the Fenners came up carrying little Tommy.

It was Tommy who started the heroine business. He had told his parents that Carly had saved him when the horses bolted. At first she tried to protest, but nobody listened, and when Tommy wanted to hug and kiss her to thank her for saving his life, she quit arguing. It was true, in a way, she decided. After all, he could have been badly hurt if she hadn't been there for him to land on when he fell off his box. So she hugged him back and told him he was very welcome. And then the Fenners went off and Carly stayed in front of the fire station with her family until the parade was over and it was time to go to the picnic grounds.

❦❦❦ *chapter 20*

The huge Fourth of July picnic at Oak Park had always been one of Carly's favorite events. There were, of course, other large group picnics in Santa Luisa. All through the spring and summer, and well into the fall, there were church and lodge and family reunion picnics at Oak Park, as well as the many state picnics when Ohioans and Missourians and Iowans got together with others who had come to California from their home states.

But the Fourth of July picnic was for everybody, and that in itself made it different and much more interesting. On that one day you could expect to meet people you weren't related to, and who didn't attend your school or church. Now and then you might even meet people you'd never seen before. That possibility in itself was intriguing. Particularly for someone who lived out in the country and who had a father who felt that most social activities were a waste of time.

There were always a great many social activities at the Fourth of July picnic. After everyone had eaten all they possibly could, there were speeches and musical offerings and a

great many games and races and contests. The celebration
lasted all through the day and at night there was more music,
the kind that people dance to. That is, some people danced,
like Catholics and free-thinkers, not to mention a few of the
more worldly Presbyterians and people like Henrietta Spots-
worth, who was a fallen-away Baptist. And of course there
were the fireworks that went off continually between and
during all the other activities, all day long and far into the
night.

But the scheduled events were not the best part of the day.
In Carly's experience the best things were the ones that nobody could plan or predict. Just like firecrackers those best
things always seemed to happen when you least expected it.

There had been the time, for instance, that Ralphie Rasmussen and Ernest Robinson tied in the hundred-yard dash
and got into a fistfight over the blue ribbon. And Ralph se-
nior punched Andy Robinson, who was Ernie's uncle, and a
Rasmussen hired man punched one of the Robinsons', and it
was all terribly exciting for a while until somebody called
Sheriff Simms.

And then, just last year, little Billy Purvis ate too much and
went to sleep under a table, and his mother put up an awful
fuss. Everybody thought he'd been drowned in the mill run
or maybe kidnapped, and the whole picnic broke up into
search parties. That had been the most exciting picnic ever—
until the Fourth of July in 1907.

Of course in 1907 the holiday had gotten off to a really
extraordinary start with the runaway float, and afterward at
the picnic things continued to be unusually exciting, at least
for Carly. As she helped carry the Hartwick picnic baskets
from the surrey to the tables, and then joined in the feasting,
she was still the center of attention. Nearly everybody she
knew stopped by to tell her how sorry they were about the

firecracker thrower and the runaway float, and how glad they were that she hadn't been injured.

Dressed now in her new blue percale dress with the square white collar and wide polka-dot sash at the dropped waistline and a hair ribbon to match, Carly sat between Lila and Aunt M. and tried to eat and answer questions at the same time. Between mouthfuls of cold fried chicken and potato salad and corn on the cob, she talked to a great many people, thanking them for their concern and answering their questions, at least the ones she could answer.

But there was one question that nobody could answer, and that was, Who had thrown the string of firecrackers under the hooves of the Quigley grays? Everyone agreed that it had been a criminally irresponsible thing to do, and whoever had done it should be caught and severely punished, and they also agreed that it was very strange that the guilty party had managed to go entirely unseen.

"No," Carly told her sympathetic listeners, "I guess I wasn't looking in the right direction. I didn't see anyone throw them, and after the trellis fell on me, I couldn't see anything at all."

It seemed that none of the parade spectators had seen the firecrackers thrown either. And Arthur, who was determined to find the guilty party, had learned that neither had any of the other Symbols of Patriotism on the Presbyterian float.

"It was almost as if those firecrackers came right down from the blue," Mrs. Jenkins said before she patted Carly's cheek for the third time and hurried off to get some more of her own famous corn soufflé before it was all gone.

Carly was as baffled as everyone else, and it wasn't until some time later, as she was finishing her apple pie and ice cream, that she just happened to recall something that seemed like an important clue. The clue had come from Brother Tupper's sermon.

Thinking, as she was, about parades and explosions, she suddenly remembered what Brother Tupper had said about bombs—bombs that had been thrown during meetings and rallys and *parades*. According to Brother Tupper the bombs had been thrown by atheists and were a part of their last-days attack on the innocent and the righteous. And while Brother Tupper hadn't specifically mentioned throwing firecrackers at Presbyterians, there certainly were some similarities.

It was a fascinating idea. With her spoon hand frozen halfway to her mouth, Carly went over the evidence—and came to a conclusion. The conclusion was that what was needed was an investigation by Sherlock Holmes and Dr. Watson—and the sooner the better. Quickly scooping up the last spoonful of ice cream, she stood up and looked around for Matt.

He couldn't have gone far. Carly had seen him only a few minutes earlier at the dessert table. In fact, she'd seen him at the dessert table at least three times. But now, when she needed him, it seemed that he'd finally had enough to eat and gone elsewhere. She would have to go looking for him—and quickly, before somebody made other plans for her.

By leaning to one side she could just see the empty spot at the hitching rack where the Hartwick surrey had been until poor Nellie left for home. That had been almost an hour ago. At any time one might expect to hear the clop and jingle of the returning horse and rig—announcing Father's arrival. The investigation, if there was to be one, would have to begin immediately.

Getting up from the table with what she hoped was a casual, unhurried air, Carly looked around for the best avenue of escape. In one direction Aunt M. was busy talking to Elvira Hopper of Elvira's Hat Shop, and in the other Lila was picking daintily at a piece of berry pie. Both Charles and Arthur had already finished eating and disappeared. Carly moved to the end of the table, put her plate and utensils in one of Nellie's baskets, and then kept moving.

Making her way down the row of serving tables, she pretended to be scanning the remaining food, as if she were looking for something more to eat. But once past the dessert table, covered now with almost empty tins and plates, she turned sharply to the left and ducked into the crowd around the horseshoe pits. Old Grundy Appleton was throwing against Grandpa Díaz, and most of the spectators were nearly as old as the contestants. She stopped for a moment to watch Grandpa Díaz pitch a shoe that missed being a dead ringer by no more than two inches.

"By jingo! Would you look at that," someone said. "Blind as a bat and he durn near throws two ringers in a row. What would the old coot do if he could see?"

"Wahoo! Go to it, Grandpa," someone else shouted, and others chimed in. "Hurrah for Grandpa!"

Excited by the general enthusiasm, Carly joined in the cheering, and her "Hurrah for Grandpa" carried unexpectedly over the deep rumble of old men's voices. Some of the men looked at her and laughed and she ducked her head and blushed, and then, encouraged by their friendly smiles, she cheered again. She liked the excitement of the match and the comfortable companionship of the crowd, with its familiar homey old-man smell of wool and starch and tobacco. She wanted to stay long enough to see if Grundy would do as well as Grandpa Díaz, but it took him so long to smooth out his pitching stand, spit on his hands, and wind himself up that she decided she couldn't wait. She ducked through the horseshoe spectators and began to run.

She would try the racing field next. Matt was a fast runner and he liked to enter races. Squeezing through a tightly packed crowd at the starting line, she checked out the runners lining up for the next race. It was a gunnysack race and the contestants were boys, all right, but too young—first and second graders. Nearby a group of young ladies, high school girls mostly, were practicing carrying potatoes on soup spoons. The starting gun went off, the little boys bounced off down the track holding the gunnysacks up under their armpits, and the young ladies moved up to the starting line.

Carly waited until the gunnysack boys had finished and been awarded their ribbons, and the young ladies had started down the track. They looked very lovely, she decided, gliding gracefully in their long skirts and frilly shirtwaists with their potato spoons carefully balanced before them. Not as beautiful as Lila would have looked, of course, if she had entered. Carly wondered why she hadn't.

Everyone laughed and cheered, and then gasped with sympathy when Edna Purvis's potato bounced out of her spoon and she left the race, wrinkling her freckled nose in disgust. Carly watched until tall, lanky Emily Stone came in first and was awarded the blue ribbon. Then, still picturing Lila receiving the ribbon—Lila, smiling her small perfect smile, her lovely head with its heavy load of hair held proudly erect—Carly left the field and moved on. She would go next to the ball field. Matt liked baseball a lot too. It was likely that he would be at the game. As it happened, Matt wasn't—but Lila was. And so was Johnny Díaz.

119

❧❀❀ *chapter* 21

The moment Carly came out of the sycamore trees that grew around the millpond, she saw Lila near the stands, with Johnny right beside her. They weren't talking to each other, at least not that Carly saw, but as she got nearer they glanced at each other and then turned away, and in a moment looked back again. It was a quick secret look, but Carly knew what it meant.

She had known the secret for a long time, ever since the warm spring night more than two years ago when she sat down by Lila on the front steps and asked her why she looked so sad—and to her surprise Lila had answered. With her chin in her hands, her face a gleaming ivory cameo in the soft moonlight, Lila began to talk, not so much to Carly as to the wide night sky. Slowly, almost as if she were talking in her sleep, she went on and on reciting every tiniest detail of the day when Johnny Díaz had told her that he loved her. Johnny had been seven years old at the time and Lila was only six, but she had been in love ever since.

Johnny Díaz was seventeen, now. He had blue-black hair

so heavy that it looked like a thick cap of curls, and his eyes were dark and sharply watchful, like the eyes of a wild colt. He had a quick white smile, a graceful, sauntering walk, and a face that Aunt M. said could "break an angel's heart." Carly thought that Johnny was too handsome to have been born in modern times. He should have lived when men wore velvet coats and plumed hats and carried shining swords at their hips. She also thought that Johnny and Lila were just exactly like Romeo and Juliet. That was because Johnny was a Díaz, and the Díazes were—different. The difference was complicated and puzzling.

The Díazes had lived in the Santa Luisa valley for longer than anyone except, of course, the Indians. Although Grandpa Díaz spoke Spanish and had come to the valley from Mexico, some people said he was not Mexican, but Spanish, and that seemed to be important. Although most of the Mexican families lived all together on the south side of town near the river, or on the ranches where they worked, Johnny's family lived at the end of Hamilton Valley on land that still belonged to them, although it had been leased for a long time. Unlike the other Mexican women, Johnny's mother and grandmother were sometimes invited to socials at Citronia and other important houses. And his father, Fernando, belonged to the Odd Fellows and the volunteer fire department.

But if being Spanish was a difference that wasn't too serious, there were others that were. For one thing the Díazes were Catholics. That would have meant trouble enough, but even more of a problem was the fact that most of the Díaz land was leased to the Quigleys. In fact, Johnny's father, Fernando Díaz, was a member of Alfred Bennington Quigley's water company and had voted against Aunt Mehitabel's request for membership and a share in the company's irrigation water. And those differences explained what happened the

121

one time Johnny had come calling on Lila. Father had sent him away and ordered Lila never to speak to that Díaz scamp again. So Johnny and Lila were not only young and beautiful and in love, but also from families that hated each other— exactly like Romeo and Juliet's.

Watching them now, reading the secrets of their silence, Carly wrapped her arms around her middle and shivered in painful ecstasy. It was all so frightening and forbidden and wonderful that it made her stomach ache. She went on watching and shivering while Johnny and Lila looked at each other several more times before she realized what a perfect opportunity was presenting itself. An opportunity for her to play a part in a love story. Springing into action, she leapt forward, almost running over two little girls playing jump rope. "Hello" she said as she skidded to a stop. "Hello, Johnny. Hello, Lila."

Both Johnny and Lila stared at her in a way that was not particularly welcoming. Almost stammering in her eagerness to make them understand her good intentions, and the value of what she was offering, she managed to say, "C-c-could I take messages? I mean, Father didn't tell me not to talk to Johnny. I mean, if you both tell me things to tell each other, then you wouldn't really be talking—to each other, that is."

Johnny rolled his dark eyes and laughed and Lila said, "Oh, for heaven's sake, Carly. Go away. Would you just go away, please?"

Carly was surprised and a little hurt. It had seemed like such a good idea. "Well, all right," she said. "I was just trying to help."

As she walked away, she looked back several times over her shoulder. Johnny and Lila still didn't seem to be talking. It was possible that people in love didn't need to—that people in love were able to read each other's minds.

It was only a minute later, as Carly was just reentering the sycamore grove, that she saw something very dangerous—for Lila and Johnny. It was Father. He had stopped to talk to someone near the millpond, but he was obviously headed for the ball game. Carly turned and ran.

Back beside Lila at the edge of the ballpark, Carly breathlessly whispered, "Father," and in a split second Johnny disappeared into the crowd of spectators. Lila didn't say thank you, but a few minutes later, as the three of them were on their way to hear the Fourth of July speeches, she looked right at Carly and smiled. It was something she didn't do very often, and it gave Carly a nice warm tingle somewhere behind her eyes. She smiled back as hard as she could.

Lila hadn't argued when Father said they were going to the speeches, but Carly had at least tried. "Don't you want to eat before you go?" she asked Father. "The food's awfully good."

Father's smile, tight and one-sided, was not a good sign. "I ate before I came. I can't understand this strange passion for eating under the open sky like savages, unless one prefers one's food seasoned by dust and insects."

Carly's next attempt had consisted of repeating some of the comments Father had made about last year's speakers, but that didn't work either.

"Don't criticize your elders," Father said, and that was that. A moment later they arrived at the bandstand.

The next day the *Santa Luisa Ledger* said that Colonel J. C. Edwards's oration abounded in eloquence, wit, and instruction, and that Miss Maudie Longworth's recitation of the Declaration of Independence was given in a most impressive and masterly manner, and that the organ, borrowed for the occasion from the music room of the Quigley mansion, was presided over with much elegance and grace by Miss Penelope Titus.

Carly supposed it was true. If she herself had failed to be

instructed and impressed, it was probably because her mind had been elsewhere. Just before the three of them had taken their places in the audience, she'd caught a glimpse of Matt hanging by his knees from the limb of an oak tree. By dropping back a few steps she'd been able to motion to him, a frantic waving of arms which she wasn't at all sure he read correctly. It had been a complicated message to send by sign language, and his face hadn't exactly lit up with understanding. But on the other hand, understanding might be hard to read on a face that was upside down. So all during the instructive speeches and elegant music, she'd been busy wondering if Matt would be waiting for her.

But when she finally managed to edge away from Father during an intermission, Matt suddenly appeared at her side.

"Sure," he said, "I knew. You were saying to wait around until you could sneak away from your pa. I knew that right off."

Carly giggled, and then, deepening her voice to a pitch more suitable for Sherlock Holmes, she said, "A brilliant deduction, Dr. Watson. Or—what was that Indian's name?"

"Eenzie," Matt said.

"A brilliant deduction, Eenzie. Come on, let's run."

They ran through the park and out onto the shortcut path to Palm Drive, where they had to stop for breath. Clutching his side, Matt said, "By hokey, you sure can run some for a girl, Carly. Where the Sam Hill we goin', anyways?"

"We're going," Carly said, "to solve the mystery of the Fourth of July Assassins."

"The Fourth of July who?" Matt asked.

"Assassins. The evil murderers who threw the bomb under the royal coach." When Matt went on looking as blank as a barn wall, she sighed and said, "Okay. That part is just pretend. But there's a real mystery, and we're going to solve it.

124

We're going to find out who threw the Big Reds at the Presbyterians. My theory is it was done by atheists."

After a minute Matt closed his mouth and grinned. "Shucks," he said. "I never heard tell of any—what did you call them?"

"Atheists," Carly said.

"Yeah. I never heard of any of them in Santa Luisa. What do they look like?"

"They don't look like anything special. But Brother Tupper—he was the visiting preacher from Carolina—Brother Tupper says they're people who don't believe in God or Congress or policemen, and they go around throwing bombs at the righteous. Some of them might live right here in Santa Luisa and we wouldn't even know because they usually act like ordinary people except they don't go to church or vote or pay their taxes."

Matt grinned. "That part sounds like my grandpa."

"Really?"

Matt stopped grinning. "He didn't do it, Carly. He don't even hold with firecrackers. He heard about a boy in Santa Barbara got his eyes put out, and since then he won't let me have anything but ladyfingers."

Carly laughed. The idea of Dan Kelly throwing firecrackers was pretty ridiculous. "I know he didn't," she said. "Come on. Let's go."

✽✽✽ *chapter* 22

When Carly and Matt reached the corner of Palm and Main, the street was deserted. Except for some scraps of paper streamers and a few more orange peels and candy wrappers than usual, there was nothing to indicate that a parade had recently passed that way—or that a tragedy had nearly happened on that very spot. Their most exciting find was a few scraps of red firecracker paper in the middle of the street.

"Big Reds," Carly said excitedly.

"That don't mean nothing," Matt said. "Lots of people have Big Reds."

Carly nodded. She picked up a few scorched shreds of paper and carefully put them in her pocket. Then she looked up and down the street. Up and down—and up again, to the second story of the Olympic Hotel. Suddenly she grabbed Matt's arm and pointed.

"Up there. The assassins must have been on the roof of the hotel. See, they could have been standing behind that false front where no one could see them, and all they had to do was light the string and toss it over."

"Yeah," Matt said. "By hokey, Carly. I bet that's it, all right."

In the lobby the clerk, Elmer Somebody-or-Other, a pale, pointy-faced young man from Ventura, was slouched down in a swivel chair with his feet up on the desk, sound asleep. Carly and Matt tiptoed past him and up the stairs. She'd never been upstairs in the Olympic before, but it wasn't hard to find the second flight of stairs and the door to the roof.

The incriminating evidence was right there, where Carly had expected to find it. On the tar-paper roof directly behind the false front, there were several burnt matchsticks and a couple of firecrackers that had obviously pulled loose from a string.

"See, I told you!" she said. "Big Reds. We've solved the mystery. We found where they, the atheists, were standing."

"Okay," Matt said, "but who are they? What do they look like?"

Carly sighed impatiently. "Like I told you, they probably look pretty much like everybody else. We've just got to get a good description of them."

"How're we going to do that?"

Carly began to shake her head, but all of a sudden she nodded instead. "I know," she said. "I know how. Let's go down and ask the clerk. Maybe he saw somebody go up on the roof."

"Maybe," Matt said. " 'Less he was asleep at the time. Reckon he wasn't, though. Not during the parade. Maybe he did see something."

Carly had started down the first flight of stairs, with Matt right behind her, when suddenly she stopped dead. Turning back, she put her finger to her lips and then squatted down behind the bannisters. Behind her Matt did the same thing. By peering out between the rungs they were able to get a clear view of the front desk, where Elmer was now wide awake and talking to a visitor. The visitor was wearing a fashionable linen summer suit and a motoring duster and his large portly shape was strangely familiar. It looked like—and it was—Alfred Bennington Quigley.

Mr. Quigley had lowered his voice from its normal booming roar to a loud hissing whisper. Carly couldn't quite tell what he was saying, but as usual it sounded very forceful. And by the eager way Elmer was nodding and shaking his head, it was easy to see that he was impressed. And then as Carly and Matt watched, Mr. Quigley reached in his pocket and counted a bunch of bills out onto the counter. It looked like quite a lot of money.

Elmer was reaching toward the money when Mr. Quigley turned to look carefully around the lobby and Carley ducked away from the bannisters, pulling Matt with her. By the time they dared to peek out again Elmer was alone, standing stiffly behind the counter with a surprised look on his pale, pointy face.

Carly and Matt waited for a few minutes and then they went on downstairs and tried asking Elmer if he had seen anybody go up on the roof during the parade. Even before they asked him, Carly pretty much knew what Elmer would say—or wouldn't say. Elmer, it seemed, hadn't seen anybody, or anything, and as far as he knew, nobody had even been near the roof of the hotel during the parade. That was what he said, but he didn't say it with much conviction, and it was perfectly clear that talking about it made him extremely nervous.

They might have tried to question Elmer a little longer, but Carly suddenly noticed the time on the big wall clock in the lobby, and grabbing Matt by the arm, pulled him out onto the sidewalk. "Run," she said. "I've got to get back right away."

They ran most of the way back to Oak Park. There was no

time—or breath—for talking. But when they were approaching the bandstand, where the final speech was just ending, Matt grabbed Carly's arm and pulled her to a stop. Grinning and gasping for breath, he said, "Well, I guess that lets the atheists off the hook, anyway."

Carly nodded. She hated to admit it. It would have been a lot more exciting if it had been atheist assassins instead of just old Henry Quigley Babcock again.

They caught sight of Carly's family then, but before Matt faded away into the crowd there was just time for Carly to warn him to keep quiet about what they had seen at the Olympic Hotel. "Don't tell anyone," she whispered. "Least not until we get some proof. But in the meantime we'll keep the suspect under observation."

"How we going to do that?" Matt asked.

"Well, maybe we'll disguise ourselves like Sherlock did sometimes so we can follow him around without him recognizing us."

Matt grinned sarcastically. "Sure thing," he said. "Sure we will."

"We will so," Carly said, jutting out her chin. "Just you wait and see, Matt Kelly. I have it all planned out. Do you want to hear how we're going to do it?"

"Later," Matt said as he started edging off among the trees. "Later. Okay?"

"Okay," Carly called after him. "And remember. Keep mum."

chapter 23

On the very next day Carly began work on a plan for a Sherlock Holmes–type investigation of Henry Babcock and his role in the bombing of the Presbyterian float. However, problems began to arise almost immediately.

She was forced to abandon her first version of the investigation because it did, in fact, depend on the use of disguises, just as she'd told Matt that it would. Carly loved the idea of disguises, of passing entirely unrecognized among friends and acquaintances—as well as suspected criminals. The difficulty was that most really good disguises, as described by Arthur Conan Doyle, seemed to require the use of a false beard.

After an attempt to make one out of mule-tail hair, Carly decided she'd have to buy one, but that proved to be impossible, too, since neither the Emporium nor Sears, Roebuck, carried false beards. And after trying the mule-tail beard with several different costumes, she finally had to admit that even a good beard probably wouldn't be very convincing on either Matt or herself.

And then it turned out that all the time Carly was working on plans and disguises for the investigation, there was another even more serious problem. One that she didn't even know about until she went up to Grizzly Flats to see Matt.

It was about a week after the Fourth when Carly managed to talk Nellie into letting her use Venus and the road cart to go up to Grizzly Flats to visit the Kellys. The trip itself wasn't easy. No trip with Venus ever was.

Venus, sometimes known as Broomstick, was an ugly old lop-eared jenny mule that the Hartwicks had had as long as Carly could remember. Besides being a biter and a balker, Venus was a stall-squasher, and that's where she'd gotten her nickname—Broomstick.

For years anyone who went into Venus's stall risked being squashed as she stepped quickly over to pin the intruder between the wall and her barrel-shaped rib cage. But then Arthur had invented a cure for stall-squashing—a broomstick. Arthur had sharpened a foot-long piece of broomstick and put it on a shelf just outside Venus's stall so it could be carried by anyone who went in. The broomstick solved the problem because after the first time Venus leaned on that sharpened point she gave up stall-squashing. But she was still a balker, and even when she was moving it was about as fast as molasses in January. Usually Carly didn't mind, because she really liked ornery old Venus. But that particular day was hot and dusty, and Carly was in a hurry to talk to Matt.

Tiger had insisted on coming along and he turned out to be a nuisance, too. He kept begging to ride in the cart, but as soon as Carly stopped to boost him up, he'd see something he wanted to chase and jump down again. And a minute later he'd be whining for another boost. Then, as likely as not, with Tiger back in the wagon, Venus would decide to balk.

By the time they arrived in Grizzly Flats, Carly was hot and tired and not in a very good mood. And the first thing Matt said to her as she climbed down from the road cart was "Don't reckon we'll be doing much of that spying stuff this summer. Leastways not on old Henry. Huh?"

Halfway out of the cart, Carly glared at Matt over her shoulder. "What do you mean?" she said. "Why won't we?"

"Reckon you haven't heard," Matt said, grinning his orneriest grin. "Old Henry's in Philadelphia."

At first Carly was sure Matt was just saying that to make her angry—and it did, all right. In fact she climbed right back into the cart and would have started for home, except that Venus balked, and by the time Carly got her started Matt had convinced her that he was telling the truth.

Henry had been sent away for the whole summer. Right after the Fourth of July picnic he'd been sent away quickly—suspiciously quickly, Carly thought—to visit his father's relatives in Philadelphia.

So that was the end of the Babcock investigation, at least for the summer. Carly was terribly disappointed, but by the time she'd had some cookies and lemonade in the Kellys' kitchen, she'd cooled off and had begun to have a good time. For a while she and Matt had fun sliding down haystacks, and later they went back into the kitchen and listened to Dan tell about grizzly bears and mountain lions and, most of all, condors. Hearing about how Dan Kelly had once spent a long time far up in the Sespe Canyon, studying a pair of condors, was so fascinating that Carly almost decided to give up being a detective in favor of condor watching. When she left Grizzly Flats that day, she promised Matt she'd let him know as soon as she could get away for another trip to Condor Spring.

As it turned out, Carly didn't get away from home much at all the rest of that summer, except of course to Greenwood, and not even there as much as usual. She didn't get to Condor Spring even once, and there wasn't much time for Sherlock Holmes either. The difference that summer was—work.

And Condors Danced

It was around the middle of July when Father called a family conference to explain how little money had been left over after the lawyer had been paid for fighting the Quigley lawsuit. Everyone, Father said, was going to have to make sacrifices. After the pitting season was over, Arthur was going to have to find a job in town, instead of going away to college as he had planned. Charles was going to have to work twice as hard during the apricot and walnut harvest so fewer hired hands would be needed. And Nellie and Lila would have to go on doing without Carmen.

"And now that you are eleven years old, Carly," Father said, "you'll be expected to do your part."

Carly's part turned out to be an awful lot of sweeping and dusting and mopping and helping with the washing and ironing. Of course she'd helped out with housework before, but only now and then. That summer of 1907 the now-and-then ended, and the everyday and almost-all-day began. And besides the housework she spent three weeks pitting apricots, standing beside endless wooden trays in the hot, dusty pitting shed, trying to keep from being bored by imagining she was somewhere else, and cutting her own thumbs almost as often as she cut the apricots.

July went by very slowly. When she wasn't working, Carly read books from Aunt M.'s library, wrote in her journal, and taught Tiger to play Sherlock Holmes.

In the game Tiger was usually Sherlock Holmes and Carly was a dangerous escaped criminal. She would make him go in the doghouse and lie down and then she would run and hide. Tiger learned very quickly to stay in the doghouse until she called, and then he would come and find her. Except that he sometimes tried to peek while she was hiding, he was an excellent and extremely enthusiastic Sherlock, but he never quite got the hang of being a criminal. He did learn to run away and hide when Carly told him to, but he always hid in the same place behind the barn, which got a little boring after a while. At least it became boring for Carly, but Tiger never stopped getting terribly excited every time she came around the corner of the barn and found him.

In August Mama had one of her bad spells, and for quite a while Doctor Dodge came to the house almost every day. Nellie seemed to be awfully worried, but when Carly asked, she only said that the doctor didn't think it was consumption. Consumption was what Mama had always thought she might die of, ever since she'd had so much trouble with her lungs when she was a young girl back in Maine. But now, even though Mama wasn't coughing like she used to, she was weak and feverish, and dizzy when she tried to walk.

For a long time everyone went around the house on tiptoe so Mama wouldn't be disturbed, and for most of August she didn't feel like talking to anyone except Nellie and Father and, of course, Doctor Dodge. But toward the end of the month Carly sometimes was allowed to carry up her dinner tray and stay awhile to talk. She always said she was "a little better," but sometimes she said she didn't feel up to talking and would Carly just read to her—usually Wordsworth or Longfellow or Elizabeth Barrett Browning. Carly didn't mind reading but she missed all the stories about Mama's childhood in the state of Maine.

All of August was hot and dry and the days seemed to last forever, but at last it was over; September started and it was time for school to begin.

❧❈❧ *chapter 24*

"Well, I never," Mavis said. "You really mean that, Carly Hartwick?"

Carly and her two closest friends—not best, necessarily, but closest geographically, since they both lived out in the country east of town—were sitting on the school steps. It was the first day of school. Mavis and Emma had arrived early in hopes of getting their pick of the desk assignments. Carly always arrived early, since Lila had to drop her off and then reach Santa Luisa High School by eight-thirty. While they waited for Mr. Alderson to open the classroom door, they were playing jacks.

"Course I do. I wouldn't have said it if I didn't mean it. I'm just real glad summer's over, that's all. I couldn't wait for school to start."

Carly couldn't help grinning, enjoying her friends' stares of shocked disbelief. She kind of liked shocking them, particularly Emma. But the fact of the matter was that she was only telling the truth. Summer had never been her favorite time, and once the Fourth of July was over, the summer of 1907

135

had turned out to be even worse than usual. So even though she might have said it anyway just to see the look on Emma Hawkins's face, Carly really meant it when she said she was glad that school had started.

After Emma stared at Carly with her mouth open for at least half a minute, she shut it again, blinked her eyes hard, and said, "I hate school. I purely hate it. And my pa says it's a plumb shame to waste time and money on schooling for females once they've learned to read and figure up the grocery bill. He says the county's got no business telling families how much schooling their children's got to have."

"It's so much work," Mavis said. "How can you like doing long division and memorizing rivers and mountains and all those dates? Oh, fudge! You made me miss, talking so much. Whose turn is it?"

"It's mine," Carly said. "I'm on my threezies." She scattered the jacks, studied them for groups of three, and tossed up the ball. "School," she said between scooping grabs, "is easy. At least it's a lot easier than washing and ironing and sweeping and beating rugs. And more fun too."

"Do you have to do things like that?" Emma asked. "Why don't you have Carmen do it? Doesn't she work for you anymore?"

Carly missed the last scattered group of three and passed the ball and jacks to Emma. "She didn't work for us at all this summer. Father said we couldn't afford it. So Nellie and Lila and I had to do everything. But now Carmen is coming back again, but just on Mondays and Tuesdays to help Nellie with the washing and ironing."

Emma pricked up her ears and stopped playing. Nellie said that the Hawkins women were all natural-born gossips. Just like her mother, Emma loved to hear news about people, particularly bad news. "Your pa still having bad luck with Miz Carlton's land?" she said with unconvincing concern. "I

136

heard my pa say that a couple more dry years would just about ruin you folks."

"No," Carly said. "Not bad luck. Just not enough water. And Carmen's not coming back because things are any better. It's just that Nellie can't possibly take care of Mama and do everything else while Lila and I are in school. So we're having Carmen back, but just for two days a week."

Emma sighed deeply. "It's a plumb shame that Mr. Quigley won't let your papa join the water company. My papa's a charter member. Why won't Mr. Quigley let your aunt and papa join, Carly?"

"I don't know," Carly said. "Just because my Aunt Mehitabel wouldn't sell him her land after my uncle died, I guess. Go on, Emma, play. Aren't you going to take your turn?"

"My papa says"—Emma face had the weasely expression it always got when she was going to say something spiteful—"that Alfred—my papa calls Mr. Quigley *Alfred*—that Alfred would have asked your pa to join a long time ago if he wasn't so cussed."

It wasn't the first time Carly had heard talk of that sort, but this time it made her angrier than usual. She could feel her cheeks and eyes getting a burny feeling. Making her burny eyes stare right into Emma's slightly bulgy ones, she said, "That sounds like something your pa would say, all right. Cussed is kind of a hill-billy word, isn't it?"

Emma's eyes glittered and her face became even more pinched and weasely. "My pa's not the only one who says that, Carly Hartwick. Everybody says your pa's the orneriest man in Santa Luisa. And that what ails your ma is mostly in her head, and—and—" Emma's voice was getting higher and squeakier and her eyes had gotten even bulgier, as if they were about ready to pop right out. For a moment Carly got so interested in Emma's condition, wondering what it felt like to be so beside yourself, that she almost forgot how angry she was herself. "—and—and—" Emma caught her breath in a rasping gasp, as if she had almost suffocated, and went on, "and all of you Hartwicks think you're so high and mighty, and—and—"

While Emma was strangling over her next insult Carly got up off the steps and said to Mavis, "I think I'll go over and watch the boys play andy over. Want to come along?"

Mavis looked from Carly to Emma's quivering red face and then she stood up, too. "I—I guess so," she said. "Yes, I guess I do."

As they rounded the corner of the schoolhouse, Mavis glanced back over her shoulder and said, "That Emma. I don't know what gets into her sometimes. Telling all those lies about your folks."

Carly shrugged and made a face. She tried to make it a who-cares kind of face, but it didn't feel right, so she covered it quickly with a grin and said, "Come on. Race you to the stump."

It was still early and only three or four boys had arrived on the school grounds, but the andy over ball was already being thrown back and forth over the top of the new outhouse. The new outhouse, or lavatory, as Miss Pruitt insisted it should be called, had been built just last year, and it was nice and modern with flush toilets and handbasins with running water. The toilets had shiny oak water-tanks up near the ceiling and a matching oak hand-grip hanging down on the end of a long chain. There were two toilets and two handbasins on the girls' side and probably two of each on the boys' side, although Carly had never seen them, of course. The new outhouse was just wide and high enough to be perfect for andy over, but when the teachers arrived the boys would have to scoot back to the tool shed, where they used to play. Mr. Alderson and Miss Pruitt thought it was indecent to play andy over, over an outhouse—even a nice new one that wasn't supposed to be called an outhouse anymore.

As Carly and Mavis climbed up to sit on the stump of the old eucalyptus tree, Will Harding, who was on the near side of the lavatory along with Luther Purdy, was just throwing the ball. "Andy over," he shouted, and tossed the ball up over the roof, and then he and Luther got ready to run. If anyone on the other team caught the ball before it hit the ground they would come dashing around the corner in a moment to try to hit Luther or Will. And, sure enough, someone did. The someone was Henry Quigley Babcock.

Skidding around the corner in a cloud of dust, Henry fired the ball at Luther, who happened to be nearest, and caught him right in the middle of the back.

"Gotcha!" Henry yelled, jumping up and down and shaking his fists. "Gotcha, Purdy."

Luther shuffled toward him, rubbing his back. "Blame it, Henry," he muttered with his face screwed up as if he were about to cry. "That hurt. Why do you have to throw so durned hard?"

As Henry Babcock strutted back toward his side of the outhouse dragging Luther with him, Carly started telling Mavis to pretend to be talking so Henry would think they hadn't noticed him clobbering Luther.

"What'll we talk about?" Mavis said, looking nervous.

"Anything," Carly said. "Recite nursery rhymes if you can't think of anything else."

So Mavis said, "Mary had a little lamb," in a self-conscious voice, and Carly made an astonished face as if she'd just heard something shocking, and answered, "Really? Well— have you heard that three little kittens lost their you-know-whats?" And Mavis laughed and said, "And you'll never guess what old Humpty Dumpty sat on." But by then Henry had disappeared back behind the outhouse, so they quit reciting and watched to see if Will would catch the ball when it came back over the roof. But at that very moment Matt Kelly rode into the schoolyard on Rosemary.

❧❀❧ *chapter 25*

The minute Carly heard the quick little trotting hooves, she jumped down off the stump and ran. She wanted to talk to Matt before he saw Henry, and to remind him to keep his mouth shut about the firecrackers and the Olympic Hotel. Matt said he hadn't forgotten but didn't see why they still had to keep mum.

"I told you," Carly said, walking along beside Rosemary as Matt led her to the horse shed, tied her up, and poured oats into the manger. "I told you, if we accuse him now, Henry'll just deny it, and we really don't have any proof yet. He'll just say his grandpa was paying Elmer for something else. And if we keep mum and hang around Henry a lot—you, that is—that's your job, and if you ask questions that get him started bragging like he always does, sooner or later he's going to spill the beans."

Matt looked doubtful. "Why is it my job?" he asked.

Carly was amazed. "Well, I can't hang around Henry, for heaven's sake. I'm a girl."

141

"Well, you're hanging around me," Matt said. "What's the difference?"

"The difference is . . . ." Carly said. "The difference is that I hate Henry Babcock."

Matt grinned a smart-alecky grin. "You don't hate me, then?" he asked.

Carly glared. "Not yet," she said. "Not yet, Matthew Kelly, but you keep acting so smart-alecky I'll get around to it for certain." Then she ran back to Mavis and the eucalyptus stump.

All the rest of the day, as school took up and Mr. Alderson, who taught fifth through eighth grade, gave his annual first-day-of-school speech, and everyone got a new desk and books and pens and pencils and got caught up on the news of the long summer during recesses and lunch hour, Carly kept one eye on Matt and Henry. Two or three times she saw Matt talking to Henry Babcock, but not for very long, and each time, afterward, he caught her eye and gave his head a tiny shake. It looked as if it wasn't going to be easy. Henry undoubtedly would have to run out of other things to brag about before he would take the risk of boasting about how he had been the one to throw the firecrackers at the Presbyterian float. Carly was prepared to wait.

When Carly ran down the schoolhouse steps that afternoon, Lila and Venus and the road cart were waiting by the gate. Carly was surprised, because she was to go to Greenwood after school and Lila usually said she could walk that far. Once in a while in wintertime when they got to use Prince, Lila would agree to take Carly to Greenwood, or even on a quick trip into town. But Lila would never agree to go anywhere extra during harvest time when Venus was the only draft animal that could be spared for the drive to school.

"I'm coming, Lila," Carly called as she jumped the last three steps and ran down the path. Outside the gate she stopped briefly to say, "Hello, Venus. Hello, old Broomstick-Venus." She rubbed the old jenny's soft nose and jerked her hand away as the cantankerous animal lifted her long upper lip and threatened to bite. Venus's good ear was flat back and the tendons on the sides of her long face quivered angrily. Carly giggled. Holding her face as close as was prudent, she crooned, "Sweet old Broomstick. Sweet old ornery Broomstick."

"For heaven's sake, Carly. Get in!" Lila said, and Carly skipped around the cart and climbed up. But when Lila flipped the reins and said, "Gee up," Venus balked.

"Oh, no!" Lila said. *"Oh, no!"* and she went on clucking and flipping the reins even though she should have known that Venus never paid any attention to that kind of thing. Once Venus began a balk, there was never anything that did any good except "the chain."

"I'll get it," Carly said, and she reached down under the seat, while Lila looked all around and then slumped down as if she were trying to hide.

"The chain" was several links of logging chain attached to a short pole. Of course no civilized person would ever hit a mule with a logging chain, but someone in Venus's long and shady past had apparently done just that, and it had made a deep impression on her. So when the stubborn old jenny went into a balk, there was nothing to do but get out the chain and shake it sharply over her back. At the very first rattle Venus would point her good ear forward and take off at a trot.

Carly thought Venus and her chain was funny, but Lila said it was mortifying. And Lila also said that Venus knew how embarrassing it was and that was why she always balked in the most public places. Lila was probably right. Venus was certainly smart enough, and mean enough, to enjoy mortifying people. So "the chain" was shaken while Lila cringed with embarrassment, Venus cocked her ear and lurched forward, and they were off and away.

All the way down Third and Arnold streets Carly asked questions and Lila answered—when she felt like it. Carly loved hearing about high school. She loved hearing about the interesting subjects that were studied there, such as civics and ethics and elocution, and she was even more fascinated by the student body, so mysteriously grown, within her own memory, from scrubby, gangly eighth graders to young ladies with high-piled hair and floor-sweeping skirts and young gentlemen with blue-tinged jaws and high celluloid collars. Lila answered three or four questions before she complained that she was tired of talking and would Carly please just sit there and keep her mouth shut. So Carly kept still, at least until Lila started to turn to the left on Hamilton Road.

"Wait," Carly said then, "I'm spending the night at Greenwood."

"You are?" Lila said. "Why didn't you tell me? I wouldn't have stopped for you."

"I know. I wondered why you did. I thought Nellie must have told you. She told me that Aunt M. had asked Father if I could."

Lila was angrily starting to pull Venus around when Carly said, "Never mind. I'll just walk from here." Putting both hands on the edge of the cart, she vaulted to the ground, and a moment later she was walking down Hamilton Road toward Greenwood.

Spending the night with Aunt M. and Woo Ying was a treat that Carly always looked forward to. Her old room, the large upstairs bedroom with the bay window that looked out over the garden, had not been changed at all since she stopped living with Aunt M. when she was not quite five years old. The Jenny Lind spool bed was still covered by the quilt appliquéd with pink rabbits, and in the corner the tiny cradle in which she had slept as a newborn was full of her baby toys.

Once when Mavis was visiting at Greenwood, she'd said it still looked like a nursery, and Aunt M. must have overheard, because afterward she suggested doing the room over so it would be more suitable for a young lady. Right at first Carly had agreed, but when it came right down to making changes, she'd found she didn't want to. Even though she seldom got to sleep there anymore, she liked thinking of the room being there, always just the same. She liked knowing it was just the way it had been when she lived there with Aunt M. and Woo Ying.

Dinner that night at Greenwood was roast chicken with almond stuffing, and there was apple tart for dessert. They ate in the kitchen so Woo Ying could eat with them, but the table was set with Aunt M.'s best linen napkins and the good china and silver, and right in the center there was such a huge bouquet of roses that you had to stand up to see the person sitting across from you. When Aunt M. saw the table, she looked surprised.

"Why are we using the company things?" she asked. Woo Ying grinned and said, "For celebrate. For very happy celebrate."

For just an instant Carly wondered if she'd forgotten a birthday or a holiday. "What celebration?" she asked. "What are we celebrating, Aunt M.?"

She halfway stood up to see over the roses and got a glimpse of Aunt M. frowning at Woo Ying and giving her head a tiny shake. Aunt M. looked down then at her plate, avoiding Carly's eyes, and for a brief moment a shadow like the ghostly wisps of a dissolving nightmare drifted through Carly's mind. It didn't seem reasonable to feel threatened by a celebration, however secret, but there'd been something unreadable and worrisome in Aunt M.'s face.

But Aunt M. smiled then and said, "Who knows? Who knows what a crazy old Chinaman will take it into his head to celebrate on a perfectly ordinary third of September? Maybe it's the kitchen god's birthday or some other nonsense."

She changed the subject then and started telling all about Abner and Elsie Stone's new motorcar that had been parked down by the train station that morning when she'd gone by on her way in to the library. It was called a Chadwick Six, or some such silly name, Aunt M. said, and it had kerosene lamps out in front so it could actually be driven at night. "Not that I'd be caught dead in one of those contraptions after dark," she said. "They're bad enough in the daytime, chugging and bouncing all over the place and sending all the horses into fits. Even my sensible Chloe, who hasn't spooked at anything since she was a filly."

Carly liked motorcars, and she was pleased to hear that the Stones had one, which made four now in Santa Luisa, unless there was one she hadn't heard about, which wasn't at all likely.

Woo Ying liked motorcars, too, and he was always trying to get Aunt M. to say they'd buy one, as soon as times got better. "Woo Ying drive," he would say, sitting down and working his hands and feet like crazy, as if there were a whole battery of wheels and rudders and levers and pedals in front of him. "Woo Ying drive and Auntie M. and missy sit in back with hats tied on so not fly away when go very fast."

All the time Aunt M. was telling about the new motorcar, Carly watched Woo Ying, hoping he'd start doing his driving demonstration, but he seemed to have other things on his mind. While Aunt M. went on and on about nearly every motorcar she'd ever seen, Woo Ying only smiled in a secretive way and nodded his head knowingly whenever Carly caught his eye.

✵✻✿ *chapter* 26

It wasn't until much later in the evening, when Carly was getting ready for bed in her old room, that she actually found out what Woo Ying had been celebrating when he set the kitchen table with the company china. She'd taken off her school dress—an old one of Lila's that had been up in the attic for four or five years waiting for her to grow into it— and was pouring some water into the basin on the dry sink when Aunt M. knocked on the door and came in. She was carrying a beautiful new summery nightgown of soft fine cotton printed with tiny blue forget-me-nots.

"Saw this on sale when I was in Finley's the other day," she said, "and it looked to be about your size." She sat down in the rocking chair then and chatted about one thing and another while Carly finished washing and got into the new gown. After a while she seemed to have run out of things to say, but she stayed where she was. It wasn't until Carly climbed into bed that she pulled the chair closer and said, "Carly, child. I don't know how you're going to feel about this, but your father has asked me if you could stay here at Greenwood this fall."

Carly stared at her aunt in astonishment. "Stay here? You mean all the time? Every day?"

"Well, during the week, at least. He said you might want to go out to the ranch on Saturdays and stay the night and then come back here after church on Sundays."

Carly opened her mouth once or twice and closed it again and then gave up on talking while a strange combination of emotions and ideas flopped around inside her head like a coopful of hysterical chickens. First of all there was delight. Not the kind of delight she might have felt when she was five and still crying herself to sleep in her dim little bedroom at the ranch house because she was lonely for Aunt M. and Woo Ying and her beautiful sunny room at Greenwood. If Mama and Father had changed their minds and let her go back to Greenwood then, her delight would have been as pure and deep as the snowdrifts in Maine.

But now there were other things to think about, like how much she'd miss out on, and how much she wouldn't be a part of, or perhaps even hear about, if she no longer lived at the ranch house. Like watching Lila and wondering about her and Johnny and their beautiful tragic love, and Arthur's exciting adventures, and the things Charles built for her, and the stories Mama told and the ones Father read on winter evenings, and Nellie's lemon cake and the way she kissed the top of Carly's head when she wanted to make up after she'd been cross.

So there was sadness mixed with the delight, and resentment that what was happening couldn't have happened five years sooner, if it had to happen at all. And there was pain, too, a vague shifting ache that she couldn't quite catch up with, and wasn't sure she wanted to. But most of all there was one word that got louder and louder inside her head, until it came out in a small breathy voice. The word was "Why?"

"Why?" Aunt M. repeated, somehow filling that one word with so much sympathy and concern that it made an unwelcome flood of self-pity and grief well up in Carly's throat and eyes. Fortunately the tears made her angry, angry to be so silly as to cry over having to live at Greenwood, and she swallowed hard and waited for the anger to burn away the tears before she said, "Yes, *why* did they decide now that I should live here when they were so sure I shouldn't when I was five?"

Aunt M.'s head tilted and her eyes drifted away for a moment before she brought them back to Carly's face. "I think you know—you must know—why they wanted you to live with them. After all, you are their child, and it was only natural for them to want you with them. The only strange part was that you had been left here with a childless old woman and a crazy Chinaman for so many years, and it would never have happened if your mother hadn't been so very ill for so long. But then when she seemed to be a little stronger, and when Nellie had gotten old enough to help care for you, it was to be expected that they would want you with them."

"But why did they change their minds now?"

Aunt M.'s eyes went quickly down to her hands, folded now in the skirt of her blue poplin. Without lifting them she began to talk, and her voice was different, more wavering and uncertain. "I'm not entirely sure except that perhaps your father feels that there's no one to supervise you adequately just now at the ranch, what with your mother's bad spell last month, and how long it seems to be taking her to get her strength back this time. I think your father feels you're at an age when you need more attention than either your mother or Nellie can give you just now, and—"

"Anyway," Carly interrupted, "you know I'm happy about

it. You know I'm as happy as—as happy as anything—to be able to stay here with you and Woo Ying. It's just that I couldn't help wondering—"

"Yes, yes. I know." Aunt M. reached over and patted Carly's hand. She was gathering her skirt to stand up when Carly said, "Aunt M. There's something else. Something that happened at school today that I want to talk to you about. Something Emma Hawkins said about Father, and the rest of us too."

Aunt M. sat back down. "The Hawkinses, is it?" she said, and suddenly her voice was back to normal, as crisp and crackly as overdone bacon. "What has that gaggle of geese been cackling about now?"

Carly couldn't help giggling. "I don't think geese cackle," she said. "But anyway—Emma got her dander up for some reason this morning while we were waiting for Mr. Alderson, and she started saying a bunch of things about the Hartwicks, like—well, first off she said that Mr. Quigley wouldn't have kept you out of the water company for so long if Father hadn't been so cussed."

Aunt M. listened quietly without interrupting, and Carly went on telling all the things Emma had mentioned, trying to keep it light and smiley, as if it didn't really matter what the Hawkinses said, since the whole family were downright famous for their spiteful backbiting. But by the time she'd finished she wasn't smiling anymore, and the angry burn was back in her eyes and cheeks just as it had been that morning.

"Well," Aunt M. said. "Well, now. I hope you didn't dignify such nonsense by arguing about it."

"No," Carly said. "I didn't. Mavis and I just got up and went down by the lavatory to watch the boys playing andy over."

"Good for you. Exactly what you should have done."

"It's not—you don't think—I mean—it's not true, is it?"

"Of course not. Not the way Emma meant it, at least. There may be a grain or two of truth mixed up in it somewhere, but not enough to worry about."

"Like what grains of truth?" Carly asked.

Aunt M. sighed. She smoothed down her skirt and examined her wrinkly old hands and sighed again. "Well," she said at last, "I think we'd have to admit that Ezra Hartwick is not the easiest man in the world to get along with."

Carly nodded, and Aunt M. nodded back and went on moving her head up and down for quite a while.

"Not without some reason," she said at last. "I'd be the first to say that Ezra's not had an easy time of it. Getting along with ordinary people never's been easy for him, and that's a fact. It's hard to say just why. He was such a bright boy. Just fifteen when I left Maine to marry Edward, but already the talk of two counties for his sharp mind and studious ways. I wasn't surprised a bit when he won the scholarship and went off to study in Boston. But somehow, things never went well for him after he came back home."

"He married Mama," Carly said. "Mama was the prettiest girl in the county and she could have married dozens of people, but she picked Father. That was one good thing that happened after he came home."

Aunt M. nodded very slowly. "Did he tell you that?"

"No. Mama did," Carly said.

"I see. Well, yes, your mama is a very beautiful woman. There's no doubt about that. And she'd been the adored and pampered only child of the wealthiest family in town. But then her father died suddenly and it turned out he'd gambled on some bad investments and most of the family's money was gone. But still, when Anna and Ezra were married, the future must have looked very bright to them. He'd just accepted the position of principal of the high school and it looked like they'd a fine life ahead of them, but somehow things didn't go well. There were misunderstandings with the school board and some of the parents, and at last he lost the principalship. And he was too proud to accept the teaching position that he'd been offered instead."

"And that's when you wrote to ask him to come here."

"Yes. And I've often wondered if things wouldn't have been better for everyone if I hadn't. I sometimes think it was selfish of me. Tearing Ezra and Anna and their five little ones away from the life they knew. And however many problems Ezra might have had as an educator, he was at least better prepared for that type of work than he was for managing a ranch in California. Your father is a very brilliant and well-educated man and it's hard for him to deal with people who are . . . well, like the Hawkinses, for instance. I'm afraid that Ezra just doesn't have it in him to be patient with people who are so proud of their own ignorance."

"But I was wondering if maybe Emma was right when she said that Mr. Quigley wouldn't have kept you out of the company if Father hadn't been so . . . cussed."

Aunt M. snorted. "Well, now. I don't know about that. Don't forget I had a little set-to with Alfred myself, first time he came pettifogging around here with his 'generous' offer for Edward's land."

Carly grinned. "I know. I've heard all about it from Woo Ying."

They both laughed and said "Aiiii!" in perfect unison. Carly, however, didn't laugh for long. "But you get into set-to's with people all the time, and the next thing you know everybody's laughing and forgetting all about it. I don't know . . ."

What she didn't know was why it wasn't that way with her father. Anyone who'd been in a set-to with Ezra Hartwick didn't forget about it, and they didn't laugh about it either.

Aunt M. sighed and shook her head. She got up slowly

with her hand on her back and went to the bay window. She looked out into the deepening night for several minutes before she came back to stand at the foot of Carly's bed. "I just wonder sometimes if they'd been better off to have stayed in Maine. There's been times, in the past, when I almost wished I hadn't asked them to come."

"But they didn't just come because you needed them. They wanted to come to California. Father says he came because he thought the climate would be good for Mama," Carly said.

"And your mother?"

"She says she came because Father needed a new start."

"Ummm!" Aunt M. said. "And, of course, no one could have known that poor little Peter was going to die, or that your mother would be so ill and—"

"Aunt M.," Carly interrupted, "Emma said that everyone says that Mama's illness is all in her head. Do you think that's true?"

Aunt M. made the harrumphing noise that meant she was really angry. "And that just takes the cake," she snapped. "Just about breaks Tildy Hawkins's record for stupid remarks —and that's going some, because she's certainly set records before in that department. Never in all my life—"

"Aunt M.," Carly broke in. "It wasn't Tildy who said it. It was Emma."

"I know, Carly. But you can be sure it came from her mother. It's not the kind of thing a child, particularly a dull-witted little thing like Emma, would think up on her own. No, it was Tildy, all right. It sounds just like her. Did I ever tell you about the time that Tildy Hawkins misunderstood something the parson said and went around telling people . . ."

She had told it before, so after a moment Carly stopped

listening. When Aunt M.'s story was over, she asked, "Then it's not true?"

Aunt M. didn't answer for a moment. When she did, her voice was very slow and soft. "No, child. I'm afraid it's not."

It was just at that moment that Carly remembered to ask about something very important. "Tiger!" she said suddenly. "What about Tiger—may he live here too?"

"Yes. Yes, of course," Aunt M. said. "I don't see any reason why not." Then she came around the bed and kissed Carly good night, pulled the blankets up around her shoulders, told her not to read too long, and went out of the room. She needn't have bothered mentioning the reading. Carly didn't read at all that night, and for quite a long time it seemed as if she might not be going to sleep either. For what seemed like hours and hours she lay wide awake, staring into the darkness, thinking and wondering and asking herself long, complicated questions that had no answers and no endings.

Some of the questions had to do with the things Emma had said, and some of them had to do with the fact that she would now be returning to live at Greenwood. It was while she was thinking about living again at Greenwood, asking herself why it had happened and what it would be like now that she was eleven years old and used to being on the ranch with the rest of the Hartwicks, that she suddenly remembered about Woo Ying and his mysterious celebration.

Of course—that was it. Woo Ying had known that she was coming back to live at Greenwood and he hadn't understood that Aunt M. didn't want it mentioned until later. Thinking about the good china and linen and the huge bouquet that he had arranged for his "very happy celebrate" made her smile, and the smile turned into a yawn that made her jaws pop. It seemed like only a few minutes later that she was waking up and it was morning and the sunlight was streaming in the bay windows of her old room at Greenwood.

chapter 27

Everything happened quickly after that. Within a few days most of Carly's clothing and personal belongings, including her books and journals and costumes, and of course Tiger, had been moved to Greenwood. Charles had even managed to get Tiger's doghouse into the buckboard and then set up again in a lovely spot under the drooping fronds of the huge old palm tree that grew beside Aunt M.'s barn.

Tiger seemed pleased when the doghouse arrived. He watched with obvious approval as Charles got it off the wagon and, with Woo Ying's help, moved it into place. As soon as the job was finished he went inside, sniffed around, and lay down briefly as if testing to see if it still felt right. But as it turned out, he didn't use it nearly as much as he had on the ranch. At Greenwood, for the first time in his life, Tiger became an indoor dog—a lawful and legitimate indoor dog, without the need to be tiptoed upstairs in the dead of night.

It began on the very first night he was there. Since Charles hadn't yet delivered the doghouse, Aunt M. told Carly to fix Tiger a bed in the tack room. The tack room, cozy and tidy and smelling pleasantly of horses and saddle leather, was one of Carly's favorite places, but Tiger didn't seem to feel the same way. Even though she made him a comfortable bed from an old saddle blanket, he gave her one of his most accusing stares, with his head dropped low and his eyes rolled up under twitching eyebrows. And not long afterward he began to complain. After he'd barked and whined for about an hour, Aunt M. told Carly to "go get that silly creature and bring him into the house."

Carly was surprised. Up until then she'd just naturally supposed that the Greenwood rules about the proper place for animals would be the same as they were at the ranch house.

"Mama doesn't like animals in the house," she told Aunt M. "I thought you probably didn't either."

"Your mama's absolutely right," Aunt M. said, scratching Tiger under his whiskery chin. "No animals in any house of mine, ever. But of course that doesn't include present company. It's perfectly obvious that Tiger is only dog on the outside. Anybody with half an eye could see that this gentleman is a lot more human than many of the two-legged creatures I've known in my day. Isn't that right, Mr. Tiger?"

Tiger rolled his eyes delightedly and wagged his tail so hard it seemed to be going in a circle.

Of course Woo Ying didn't approve. "Greenwood not animal house," he said, shaking his head and pursing his lips. "Woo Ying not keep house for animal. You want live with animal, why not bringing also Chloe and Dolly-cow. Also chickens. If Greenwood animal house, why not bringing all animals?"

At least that's what Woo Ying said on the first day, and not just once either. As a matter of fact he said it regularly three or four times an hour and he and Aunt M. had several shouting matches about it, and Aunt M. finally yelled that if he mentioned Chloe and Dolly one more time he could just go out and live in the cowshed himself. And Woo Ying said all right he would. Right after dinner he would go out and live in the cowshed. He didn't, though, and by the second or third day he was patting Tiger's head when he thought no one was looking, and slipping him chicken tails and ham trimmings.

That first week at Greenwood went quickly. Carly continued to see Lila briefly on the way to school. It hadn't been easy to talk Lila into stopping by for her. It was true, just as Lila said, that the grammar school was a very short walk from Greenwood, but Carly had other reasons for wanting the morning ride in the Hartwick road cart.

"So I won't be so homesick," Carly told Lila. "So I can at least see you and Venus every day and hear all the news from the ranch and everything."

"News?" Lila said. "News from the ranch? I can't imagine what you think there'll be to tell. How many eggs the hens laid yesterday, and how many pints of tomatoes Nellie put up?"

"Yes," Carly said enthusiastically before she realized that Lila was being sarcastic. Then she said, "Yes," again—defensively. "Why not? I like to hear that kind of news. And how Arthur's doing at the store, and how Mama is."

Lila shrugged, and then relented. "Well, all right. But be sure you're ready when I come by. Particularly after school. I hate sitting out there in front of everybody in this disgraceful old rig."

"I know," Carly said, grinning and petting Venus's nose just above her evilly lifted lip. "In this disgraceful old cart pulled by this disgraceful old lop-eared Venus. Don't worry. I promise I'll be ready."

So Monday through Friday it was Greenwood and Aunt M. and Woo Ying and school, with only a few minutes twice a day with Lila and Venus to remind Carly that she was still a

157

Hartwick. But the reminding seemed important. Without it, it was as if Greenwood mornings at the kitchen table with so much talking—most of it by Carly, since both Aunt M. and Woo Ying were always asking questions—and evenings in the parlor with Tiger stretched out on the Chinese rug while Carly read or did homework and Aunt M. read or crocheted —and the little bedtime treats that Woo Ying always had ready in the kitchen—and trips with Aunt M. to the shops and library while Woo Ying went off to visit his Chinese friends on Second Street—and all the constant talking and arguing and shouting and laughing—with all of those things filling up Carly's time and thoughts, it was easy to forget to think about the ranch house and the people who lived there and who were, after all, her real family.

But on Saturdays everything changed. Every Saturday morning Carly and Tiger got up at six o'clock and walked out to the ranch. They usually arrived in time for Carly to help Nellie fix Mama's breakfast and carry it upstairs. Ever since her bad spell in August, Mama hadn't been coming down for meals or even to spend part of the day on the parlor sofa as she had always done before.

"I rest better here," she told Carly one Saturday as she ate a tiny bit of the toast and poached egg Nellie had fixed for her. "And Doctor Dodge says I shouldn't climb stairs until I've gotten over these dizzy spells."

Carly had read about dizzy spells. In Aunt M.'s subscription magazines and Sears, Roebuck novels such afflictions were usually symptoms of mysterious illness. Although they seemed quite common in stories and novels, she had never experienced one herself except for the kind brought on by twirling in circles, which probably didn't count.

Curled up in the big rocking chair by the window, Carly thought about dizzy spells and other interesting symptoms and watched Mama reclining in the big old sleigh bed. Cradled in a great nest of pillows, with her long dark hair loose around her shoulders, she looked exactly like one of those beautiful but tragic heroines. In the novels the women in question were usually suffering from broken hearts or other tragedies, just as Mama suffered over Petey's death and the loss of her family and friends in Maine. But in the novels no one ever suggested that such illnesses were "only in her head."

A lump came up in Carly's throat and her eyes flooded with tears, hot tears that were more angry than sad. If those Hawkinses could only see Mama now, so pale and weak in her nest of pillows, they would surely take back their insulting comments. Well, never mind that bunch of cackling geese. Swallowing tears and anger, she began to ask questions of the sort that usually started Mama talking and helped to cheer her up. But this time the questions went unanswered, at least for quite a while.

Carly began by asking about the old days in Maine. After each question she watched carefully for Mama's eyes and voice to brighten as they always did when she talked about her childhood. But today she only nodded weakly, leaned back among her pillows, and let her eyes fall shut. But then Carly remembered to ask about the Mayday party.

"How many children do you have to have to weave a Maypole?" she asked, and at last Mama opened her eyes and began to tell about the Mayday party her parents had given for her on the huge lawn that stretched from their grand brick house all the way down to the river. And how all the children had danced around the Maypole weaving lovely pastel ribbons in and out to form an elaborate pattern of pinks and blues and pale yellows. Mama was looking much less weak and sad by the time Nellie came in to take away the tray with the half-eaten breakfast. But Nellie didn't mention the improvement. Instead she only insisted that Carly should come downstairs and let Mama rest.

After Nellie went out, Carly stopped at the side of the bed to kiss Mama good-bye. As always Mama turned her cheek and closed her eyes for Carly's kiss, and afterward she kept them closed. She looked very fragile and beautiful with her thick lashes dark against the feverish flush on her thin cheeks. Carly felt a hollow kind of ache and then a strange rush of anger.

"Mama!" she said sharply. "Look at me."

Mama's eyes opened. "Yes?" she said. "What is it, child?"

Carly wanted to say it again. *Look at me. At me, Mama.* But instead she only sighed and bit her lip. After a moment she said, "I liked hearing about the Maypole."

Mama nodded. "That's nice. Now you run along, dear, with Nellie. I'm feeling very tired."

Nellie was not in a good mood that day. She continued to be distant and preoccupied as Carly helped her pick string beans and tomatoes in the garden and a few late peaches from the kitchen orchard. Whenever Carly asked a question, her answer was brief and impatient, as if she had more important things on her mind. Sometimes, when she didn't know Carly was looking, a sudden grimace twisted her face, making it look pained and sad. If it had been Lila, Carly would have thought instantly of doomed romance and star-crossed lovers. But with Nellie it didn't seem likely that tragic love was involved. As far as Carly knew, there was only Clarence, and while he did have those unfortunate teeth, there wasn't anything really tragic about him.

After dinner, during which Father discussed women's suffrage and what a mistake Finland was making in allowing women to vote, and Arthur disagreed and started an argument, Carly went to bed in her old room. It was always a strange feeling to be there again after a whole week at

Greenwood, and she woke up often with odd bits and pieces of uneasy dreams floating rapidly away into oblivion. That particular night it was even harder than usual to get to sleep, and at last she got up and tiptoed downstairs to get Tiger.

Now that his doghouse was at Greenwood, Tiger had to sleep in the barn on Saturday nights. But that didn't prevent him from hearing the back door open, just as he always had, and in just a moment he was in her arms and being tiptoed upstairs. With his warm little body a comforting weight on her feet, she finally fell sound asleep and barely woke up in time to sneak him down and out the back door before Nellie arrived in the kitchen.

❀❀❀ *chapter 28*

The hot, dry month of September ended and midway through October the first of the winter rains fell, a steady downpour that turned the brown hills to fresh, new green, and filled the deeper canyons and barrancas with lush growths of fern. In between the sudden drenching rains the weather was warm and the air a clean, sharp blue. It was soon after the rains began that Carly started to ride Chloe, Aunt M.'s bay mare, to the ranch on Saturday mornings.

Chloe was saddle-broken and gentle but eager and frisky and a lot more fun to ride than old Prince. Especially since Aunt M., who thought sidesaddles were dangerous and silly, let Carly use her Princess saddle, which was made for ladies who, like Aunt M., rode astride. Carly had ridden Chloe before when she was visiting at Greenwood but she was really surprised when Aunt M. suggested she could use the mare for her Saturday trips to the ranch.

"Won't you need her here?" she asked.

"Not a bit," Aunt M. said. "I'm not much of a Saturday-night gadabout anymore. And Woo Ying never uses the rig when he goes in to visit his friends at the laundry. I worry about you going all that way alone every Saturday morning. That road's a quagmire this time of year, and besides, I hear there's been some more trouble with hydrophobia out Fillmore way. Little girl on her way to school was bitten by a rabid skunk. I'll feel better with you on horseback. You just be sure to get back here in time for church on Sunday mornings."

The first day that Carly rode to the ranch was very exciting. Wearing a divided skirt, cut down from an old one of Aunt M.'s, she set out up the valley road, riding tall in the saddle. Riding astride made it very easy to maintain a firm seat, and before she reached the ranch she tried a trot, a canter, and even, for a brief stretch on the straight road near the cemetery, an exhilarating all-out run. She had quieted the mare to a sharp high-stepping trot, and Tiger had caught up and was running alongside yipping with excitement, when she arrived at the ranch house and came face-to-face with Father.

When she rounded the curve in the drive, there he was only a few yards away, talking to Charles. Carly pulled Chloe to a quick stop. "Uh-oh!" she whispered under her breath. "Here it comes." She had known it was going to sooner or later, but she'd been hoping to put it off for a while by arriving at the house when Father was somewhere else. She waved and smiled, and reined Chloe toward the barn, trying to look unconcerned, as if everybody rode astride and wore divided skirts. Which many fashionable ladies did, as matter of fact, but which would not be a good argument to use with Father. But at a sharp "Come here, Carly," she sighed and turned back.

Father's eyes ranged over Carly and Chloe for a long time, his eyebrows tangling over his nose, before he asked if Aunt Mehitabel had purchased another carriage horse, or if she was planning to do without one on weekends to make it possible for Carly to ride a distance that she was perfectly capable of walking.

"Aunt M. says she hardly ever needs the surrey on Saturday, and I'll be back in time for church. I told her that I could walk, but she said the roads are too muddy."

"I should think a pair of storm rubbers would be a better and simpler, and more ladylike, solution," Father said, glaring at the divided skirt.

"And besides," Carly said, "she's worried about hydrophobia."

Father's eyebrows parted and rose halfway up his forehead. "Ahh!" he said, in the sarcastically patient tone of voice that he always used when someone was being particularly ridiculous. "And now, according to our authoritative aunt, one can acquire hydrophobia by getting one's feet muddy?"

"No. That's not it. It's that Mr. Purdy says that there's been some more cases of hydrophobia up the valley. Sheriff Simms had to shoot a mad dog and two skunks. Aunt M. says I'd be safer on Chloe if I met a mad dog on the way here."

So Father said he hadn't heard anything about mad dogs in the valley, but he supposed there was no arguing with hysterical old ladies and that Carly was to put Chloe in the stall next to Prince's and get out of that unladylike costume immediately. After that he didn't say anything more about it, so Carly went on riding to the ranch on Saturdays, but she was always careful to get Chloe into the barn and herself out of the divided skirt as quickly as possible.

October was almost over and the rains had stopped for a while and the sun had gone soft and gentle with Indian summer when Matt suggested another exploring trip. Carly had stopped him as he came out of the schoolyard leading Rosemary, to ask for a report on the Henry Babcock case. There was, it seemed, nothing to report. Henry was still bragging, but not about throwing firecrackers at floats, and Matt was getting bored with trying to be a spy. Exploring, he said, was a lot more fun than detecting.

Carly was in the mood to agree. Thinking about Carlton Valley and the Condor Spring, with everything awake and stretching after the fall rains, she was seized with a sudden yearning for a long ride into the hills. "All right," she told Matt. "We'll go up to the spring. We'll get an early start and go right to the spring without stopping, and maybe this time we'll get to see the condors dancing."

Matt grinned. He gathered up the reins of Rosemary's hackamore and jumped up to hang on his stomach across the donkey's back. Swinging a leg over, he sat up, still grinning. "When?" he asked.

"When?" Carly repeated. "Well, how about . . ."

A minute or two passed before Matt asked again, "Well—when?"

"Hush," Carly said. "I'm thinking." What she was thinking was that Father had said that he was going to Ventura on Friday to see the lawyers and he wouldn't be back until Saturday night.

"Saturday," she said, nodding. "Yes. I think next Saturday will be the perfect day. I'll get out to the ranch real early, and after I visit with Mama I'll ask Nellie, and I bet she'll let me go. She doesn't seem to care much what I do lately. You be there behind the tool shed with the donkeys by ten o'clock. Will that be all right?"

Matt said yes, it would, and so it was decided.

><del>※</del>◈ *chapter* 29

The weather was perfect on that Saturday morning. It was calm and cool with a mild, hazy sun when Carly left Greenwood for the ranch and then, if everything went well, to go on to Condor Spring with Matt. She waved good-bye to Woo Ying, who had helped with the saddle, and set off down the drive with Tiger bouncing around almost under the mare's hooves in his excitement. As if she, too, were excited by the beautiful day, Chloe tugged hopefully at the bit and danced sideways, asking to start their run early. But Carly held her in, patting her neck and explaining that it would be best to wait until they passed Arnold Street, where someone might happen to see them, and then might happen to mention to Father that his youngest daughter had been behaving like a wild thing again.

After the mare had settled into her quick, swinging walk and Tiger into his usual quest for exciting smells, first on one side of the road and then the other, Carly had time to think about the day ahead. It was such a perfect day. She felt certain that if she were ever to be a witness to the dance of the condors, it would be on a day like this. Looking westward toward the crests of the Sespe Mountains, she searched the clear blue sky for dark, soaring wings.

She began to daydream, picturing the huge birds coming in, one after the other, to land with a great rush of wind and rustle of enormous feathers while she and Matt crouched behind the ferns only a few feet away—picturing the dance, with the gigantic birds bobbing and weaving in a stately minuet, their great red heads held high and their tremendous wings outstretched—picturing birds as tall as she was, taller even, with huge curved beaks and wise and kindly eyes. She was still picturing when Tiger barked sharply, Chloe sidestepped in alarm, and Carly came back to reality to find herself almost to the cemetery gate and directly opposite a big eucalyptus tree that grew up out of the roadside ditch. Leaning against the tree, with a big red kite swinging from one hand, was Henry Babcock.

Carly reined Chloe to a stop, and as the mare sidled uneasily, she looked down at Henry and he looked back. For what seemed like forever they went on silently staring. It seemed that Henry didn't want to be the first one to speak.

"This is ridiculous," Carly said at last. "Hello, Henry Quigley Babcock. Cat got your tongue?"

"Hello yourself, Mehitabel Hartwick," Henry said with a wicked grin.

"Yes." Carly nodded, smiling calmly. "Mehitabel. There've been a lot of Mehitabels in the Carlton family. I like being a Mehitabel."

"I'll bet," Henry said. "Then why do you call yourself Carly?"

"Because Aunt M. says one Mehitabel at a time is enough. She was the one who started calling me Carly."

"Guess your folks thought she'd leave you lots of money if they named you after her. Only thing is, she's not going to have a red cent to leave anybody if she doesn't get some sense into her head."

Carly knew what Henry meant. He meant Aunt M. should get some sense into her head and sell her land to his grandpa. It was a subject that she wasn't going to get into. Not with old Henry Babcock, anyway. "Guess you're going to the High Table," she said, changing the subject. The High Table was a stretch of flat country between two ridges. The fact that there were no trees on the high flat land, and an almost unfailing ocean breeze, made it a favorite kite-flying spot.

Henry glanced down at his kite. "Yeah. Me and Bucky. He was supposed to meet me here half an hour ago." He motioned up the valley with one thumb. "You see him, tell him to get a move on."

It was definitely more of an order than a request, and all at once Carly felt the familiar fever in her eyes and cheeks. Without intending to she jerked on the reins so that Chloe tossed her head and danced sideways. Tiger moved in closer and began to growl.

"All right, Henry Babcock. I'll tell Bucky. And while I'm telling things, maybe I'll tell him that I know who threw the firecrackers at the Presbyterians. And I might even tell him that I know who paid the hotel clerk to keep mum about it. Shall I tell him that, Henry Babcock?"

For just a moment Henry looked stunned and Carly had to struggle against a triumphant smile that wanted to spread across her face. But then he shrugged and curled one side of his mouth in a scornful grin. "You can say whatever you want to. I don't care one way or the other. Nobody in this town's going to listen to a Hartwick telling tales about a Quigley, now, are they, Carly Hartwick?"

Chloe was dancing again and Tiger was crouched down, rear end in the air, yipping angrily in Henry's direction. "Come on, Tiger," Carly said. "He's not worth biting. Here,

Tiger! Come!'' She loosened the reins and started off up the road at a trot. She had gone only a few yards when she heard Henry scream.

Her first thought was that Tiger had bitten him, even though he'd never bitten anyone in his entire life, but then she saw that Tiger was right there by Chloe's hind feet. And back near the eucalyptus tree Henry was backing across the road, staring toward the bushes that grew beside the cemetery fence. Coming up out of the bushes was—a coyote.

Carly knew what it meant immediately, and Henry clearly did too. No coyote would come out onto the valley road in broad daylight when humans were around. Not unless it was mad. Then Henry screamed again and the wild-eyed, wet-jawed animal began to run, with a strange stiff-legged gait, directly toward him.

Then everything seemed to happen at once. Henry went on screaming and someone else screamed, too, a strange rasping voice that turned out to be Carly's own. ''Run, Henry. Run,'' the voice shrieked. Chloe reared and plunged. And then, as if from out of nowhere, something charged down the road and into the coyote with such force that in the collision both animals rolled down the slope into the ditch. Then Henry was running toward Carly and she kicked her foot out of the stirrup and he got his into it, and struggled onto Chloe's back behind the saddle. Chloe was running then and Henry was hanging on to Carly so hard that she could barely breathe and yelling in her ear to go faster.

She must have known immediately that it was Tiger. Her eyes and mind must have known from the first instant that Tiger had attacked the mad coyote. But fear, or shock, or Henry's screaming in her ear, must have kept her mind from turning the knowledge into understanding until they had gone a long way down the road. But all at once she was whispering, ''Tiger!'' and then screaming it, and pulling

Chloe to a stop so quickly that Henry was thrown forward, almost knocking her out of the saddle. Leaning out around him she looked back just in time to see Tiger rounding the corner at top speed. In a moment he was alongside wagging his tail and prancing with excitement.

He looked so pleased with himself and so proud of what he had done, and from up there on Chloe's back he seemed to be perfectly all right. It wasn't until they reached the ranch house that they noticed the small bloody wound on his front leg.

❧❧❧ *chapter 30*

They shut Tiger up in an empty chicken run. Carly wanted to wash his leg and paint it with Sears, Roebuck Microbe Killer or soak it in Epsom-salts water, but Nellie and Charles wouldn't let her.

"You mustn't touch him," they said. "Promise you won't touch him or let him touch you. Promise, Carly."

They were all in the kitchen by then—Nellie and Lila and Charles and, of course, Carly and Henry Babcock. Charles kept trying to take the bottle of Microbe Killer away from Carly, but she wouldn't turn loose of it.

"I have to," she yelled at them. "I have to. If we do it soon enough, maybe it will help."

But they all went on saying she couldn't. And Nellie kept telling them to lower their voices down so Mama wouldn't hear, and Henry kept asking someone to take him home to Citronia.

Henry's face was tear-streaked and his mouth quivered when he talked, and he seemed so unlike himself that it was hard to remember that he was Henry Babcock Quigley. First

171

he asked if he could ring up and ask his grandpa to come and get him, but when they reminded him that there was no telephone service in the valley, he began to ask to be taken home. "I want to go home," he said over and over. "Please somebody take me home."

But Father had Prince and the surrey and Arthur had gone into town on Comet, so that left nothing but the mules and either a buckboard or the old road cart and, of course, Chloe. Charles didn't want to use the buckboard. Although he and Henry would be safe enough up in the wagon, a mad coyote might very well attack the mules. Critters with hydrophobia would attack anything, no matter how big, Charles said, and the Hartwicks just couldn't afford to risk losing a mule. At last it was decided that Charles would take Henry home on Chloe and then go on to the sheriff's.

"And the vet's too," Carly pleaded. "You'll ask Doc Booker to come, won't you? He'll know what we should do for Tiger. Won't he, Nellie? He'll be able to give him the Pasteur treatment, won't he?"

Nellie said she didn't know what the veterinarian could do, but Charles promised to see him anyway. "Don't w-w-worry, Carly," he said as Henry climbed up behind him on Chloe's back. "I'll see the d-d-doc. He'll p-p-probably come right out and take c-c-care of Tiger."

After they'd gone, Carly went out and sat by the chicken run and talked to Tiger. She had to promise first, on her word of honor, to stay at least two feet back from the fence, and even after she'd promised, Nellie kept coming out on the back porch and checking to see that she wasn't forgetting. So she sat on an apple crate just outside the fence and talked to Tiger and waited and watched for the veterinarian to arrive.

Carly kept telling him what a good dog he was, and what a grand thing he'd done, and how much she loved him, but it was hard to tell how much he understood. He listened to what she was saying with his head cocked on one side, and wagged his tail hopefully, but when she stopped talking he began to whine and stood up on his hind legs and scratched at the chicken wire gate with both front feet.

It was all so cruel and unfair. Tiger had been tied up now and then to keep him from following people, but he was never shut up in a chicken pen except when he'd been bad. Like once when he'd dug out Nellie's iris bulbs, and another time when he'd chewed up one of Father's rubber boots. And now when he'd been a hero and saved Henry Babcock from the mad coyote, he'd been shut up again, just as if he'd done something to be punished for. It was all so unfair that it made Carly want to scream and kick things—or open the gate and pick Tiger up and comfort him no matter what anybody said. She wanted to terribly—but all she did was sit there and watch for Charles and Doc Booker.

By nine o'clock the sun was beating down on the chicken run and on Carly, too, and after a while Nellie came out carrying the big old straw hat she wore for gardening. Tiger, who had stopped scratching and was lying down with his chin on his front paws, got excited all over again when he saw Nellie, as if he thought she might be coming to forgive him for whatever he'd done wrong. He began to tear around the narrow pen in tight little circles, yipping excitedly, stopping every now and then to see if Nellie and Carly were watching. Nellie stood beside Carly for several minutes and then she put the hat on Carly's head and patted her shoulder and went back into the house. Just before she went, Carly heard her catch her breath in a strange way, but she went off then so quickly that Carly wasn't sure whether it had been a sob or only a sigh.

Carly was still sitting on the apple crate when someone said, "What'd he do this time?" and there was Matt standing right behind her. She'd forgotten so completely about Matt and the exploring trip that for just a moment she couldn't think what he was doing there. But then she remembered and started telling him the whole story, and before she'd hardly finished he said, "Lordy," and took off at a run. Carly ran after him and rounded the corner in time to see him jumping up on Rosemary.

"Where you going?" Carly yelled, and Matt yelled back, "To get my grandpa." And he swatted Rosemary with the ends of the reins and took off at a rocking gallop.

Dan Kelly, Carly thought. Of course, Dan Kelly. And for just a minute the terrible weight of pain and fear that she'd been struggling against lightened a little and she drew a deep shivery breath and felt her lips twitch in an almost smile. Of course Dan Kelly. Nobody in the whole valley, maybe even in all of Santa Luisa, knew as much about animals as Dan Kelly. Why hadn't she thought of it before?

Matt must have galloped poor Rosemary all the way to Grizzly Flats, because it was barely an hour later when he and Dan pounded down the driveway on Wilbur, one of Dan's long-legged old mules. Wilbur was all lathered up and puffing hard. Dan got a little leather case out of the saddlebag, and then he told Carly to take Wilbur out on the driveway and walk him around to cool him down.

"Your sister got a fire going in the range?" he asked, and headed for the back door without waiting for an answer. "Go on," he yelled over his shoulder as he went up the stairs. "Take that mule out and walk him and don't come back until I come get you."

"You're not going to hurt him, are you?" Carly called, running after him.

Dan smiled. "No more than I have to, lass. I'm going to cauterize the wound."

"I'll help," Carly said.

"No, lass. Matt will help me. You get on with cooling down old Wilbur. Off with ye, now. Scoot!"

Carly did as she was told. She walked Wilbur until he was good and dry, and as she walked she thought and worried and listened, but for a long time she heard nothing at all. Then there was one sharp, short yelp and soon afterward Matt came running to say that it was all over.

"Will he be all right now?"

Matt sighed. "Dunno for sure," he said. "Grandpa says it would have been better if it'd been done sooner. Like right after he was bitten. Grandpa says he saved a horse once by cauterizing the wound. A mad dog jumped out of some bushes and bit this Morgan gelding he was riding before he realized what was happening. He had his rifle along, so he shot the dog and got right off and started a fire. Had the wound cauterized inside of half an hour, and that horse never, got hydrophobia. Grandpa says he saved that horse's life for sure and all the thanks he got was just about getting his head kicked off when he did it." Matt shook his head. "Not Tiger, though. Didn't even try to bite. He seemed to know we were trying to help him."

Carly looked up at the sky. The sun was almost directly overhead. It had been four, maybe five, hours since Tiger was bitten. Still looking up into the soft blue sky, Carly silently said, "Let it be soon enough. Dear God, please let it be soon enough for Tiger."

Nellie gave Dan and Matt some lunch in the kitchen and Carly came in and tried to eat, too, but she wasn't hungry. Matt must have known that she didn't feel like going exploring, because he never even mentioned what they'd been planning to do. After they'd eaten, Dan and Matt got on Wilbur and left for Grizzly Flats and Carly went back out to the apple crate by Tiger's pen.

❧❧❧ *chapter 31*

It was midafternoon before Charles returned from Santa Luisa. He was still riding Chloe and went directly to the barn. Carly was running after him when she met Nellie, who was hurrying toward the barn from the house, drying her hands on her apron. While Charles unsaddled the tired mare, fed her, and started rubbing her down, he told them what had happened.

He and Henry had made it back into Santa Luisa, he said, past the cemetery and the place where Henry's red kite was still lying in the middle of the road, without seeing any sign of the coyote. He'd left Henry off at Citronia, and then ridden on to the sheriff's office, and Sheriff Simms had asked him a lot of questions, and then he'd called up some of his deputies. Before Charles left, the sheriff and Ralph Rasmussen and Josh Higgins had started off armed with rifles to search the area around the cemetery.

After that Charles had gone on to Doc Booker's, but the veterinarian had been out at the Robinsons' place taking care of a sick cow. Charles had waited awhile and then he'd gone on out toward the Robinsons' and met the vet on his way back into town. By then it was almost noon and Doc Booker said it would be almost another hour before he could grab a bite to eat and get out to the Carlton ranch.

"He s-s-said there wasn't anything m-m-much he could do for Tiger," Charles said in his tight, stuttery voice. He thought for a while and then went on. "S-s-said if he'd been right there when it h-h-happened, he might have tried cauterization or amputation, but he didn't see the p-p-point so many hours afterward. He asked me if I knew for s-s-sure that my pa would be willing to p-p-pay for a trip out to our place to try to s-s-save a little dog, when it might all be w-w-wasted effort anyway."

Then Nellie told Charles about what Dan Kelly had done and how Dan had also said that cauterization sometimes worked if it was done soon enough, but it wasn't for sure.

"But what about the Pasteur treatment?" Carly said. "It's for sure, isn't it? Did you ask Doc Booker about the Pasteur treatment?"

Charles nodded. "I asked. D-d-doc said it was only for humans. S-s-said vets didn't do it and he'd never heard of giving the sh-sh-shots to any animal, leave alone a little m-m-mutt dog."

Carly stared at Charles with hot eyes. Then she whirled around and started back toward the chicken run. After a few steps she stopped and turned back. "I hate him!" she screamed. "I hate him. I hate Doc Booker."

She was still sitting on the box a little later when she heard the sound of a horse and carriage in the driveway and caught a glimpse of two familiar people and an unfamiliar horse. It was Aunt M. and Woo Ying, all right, and Aunt M.'s surrey, but the horse was a beautiful dapple-gray.

She ran to meet them and they all went into the kitchen out of the hot afternoon sunshine and talked in low voices so as not to bother Mama. Carly and Nellie started telling about everything that had happened, but they soon found out that Aunt M. and Woo Ying already knew about Henry and the coyote and what Tiger had done. Aunt M. had found out about the coyote from Alfred Bennington Quigley himself.

It seemed that Alfred Quigley had arrived at Greenwood on foot a little before noon. He had come, he said, to borrow some of Aunt M.'s nerve medicine because his grandson had nearly been bitten by a mad coyote. Henry was all right, Alfred Quigley said, but Henry's mother, Alicia, was having hysterics. But then he asked Aunt M. if she knew how Carly was, and Aunt M. told him that as far as she knew her great niece was just fine, but if Alfred knew any reason why she might not be he'd better spit it out before she shook it out of him. So he told her all about what had happened.

"Seemed right unsettled, Alfred did," Aunt M. said. "Nervous-like. Almost human. Wouldn't be surprised if the real reason he came was to be sure I knew."

"That was good of him," Nellie said.

"Humph!" Aunt M. tossed her head. "Not overly. Considering there'd have been a telephone to tell both of us about the danger to our loved ones if he hadn't kept the lines from going up the valley."

Then, while Woo Ying was getting the nerve medicine, Alfred Quigley had asked if there was anything he could do, and Aunt M. said yes, he could lend her a horse because her mare was out at the ranch and she had no way to get out there. So Mr. Quigley said he thought he could take care of that and he went on home. And a few minutes later the Quigley hired man had shown up leading one of the Quigley grays.

Aunt M. wanted Carly to come home with her to Greenwood, but Carly didn't want to go. Finally they left without her and she went on sitting on the apple crate next to Tiger's pen until twilight, when Father came home from Ventura. Nellie came out to meet him, and after they'd talked he came over to the chicken run and stood beside Carly for a long time before he said anything. Then he put his hand on her shoulder and said, "I'm very proud of you, daughter, and of Tiger."

When Tiger heard Father say his name, he got up and moved quickly to the gate and stood there looking hopeful.

"Whatever happens," Father went on, "you'll always know that Tiger was a real hero, and true heroes are very rare. Emerson says, 'Heroism feels and never reasons and therefore is always right,' and that applies exactly to what Tiger did today."

Carly didn't answer. She wanted to say that she didn't care if Tiger was a hero or not, she just wanted him to be all right. But all she did was nod, and when Father took her by the shoulders and lifted her up off the apple crate, she whispered good night to Tiger and let herself be led back into the house.

❋❋❋❋ *chapter 32*

Carly went on living at Greenwood. She didn't want to, but everyone, Aunt M. as well as all the Hartwicks, insisted. But on Saturdays as well as two or three weekday afternoons after school, she rode out to the ranch to visit Tiger in his pen.

It seemed so ridiculous that she still wasn't allowed to touch him. "He's not going to bite me," she told Nellie. "Look how's he's acting. You know a dog that acts like that is not going to bite anyone."

But Nellie would only shake her head. "It's not just biting," she said. "So little is known about hydrophobia. The microbes might be in his saliva long before he shows any symptoms. And just a little lick on your finger could . . ." She grabbed Carly and hugged her fiercely and then turned around quickly to hide the tears in her eyes. So Carly ran after her and hugged her back and promised again to stay two feet back from the wire fence.

Charles had fixed up the old chicken shed at the end of the run for a shelter for Tiger, and after a while he built one for Carly too. Carly's wasn't much more than a lean-to with three side walls, but it shielded the apple crate from the sun, and a little later from the rain. It came in especially handy in December when the rainy season began in earnest.

Tiger was always glad to see her when she came visiting—or almost always. Once in a while he had a sulky spell when she first arrived and would only sit in the corner of his pen with his back to her. But he kept glancing back at her with his head low and his eyes rolled up accusingly, and after a few minutes he would cheer up and come to the gate bouncing and wagging his tail as usual. Sometimes he said hello by running in tight circles and other times he would go through all his tricks one after the other. He sat up and rolled over and played dead dog and danced on his hind legs and in between every trick he stopped to watch Carly and see if she might be so pleased that she would forgive him and let him out of prison. And over and over again she tried to explain to him why she couldn't.

Carly knew now exactly why she couldn't and what a terribly long time it would be before there was any possibility that she could. Soon after Tiger had been shut up, she had gone to the Santa Luisa library and read everything she could find on hydrophobia. She knew now that the incubation period, the time that elapsed between the bite and the beginning symptoms of the disease, could be anywhere from a month to six months. So it would be a long time, six months at least, before Tiger could be pronounced out of danger.

She also had read about the terrible course of the disease and the fact that no one, no person and no animal, had ever survived once the symptoms had begun. Once the disease started, the end was very near, because death invariably came after three to five days of terrible suffering. But as long as there were no symptoms, no strange, frightened, and restless behavior, no hanging jaw and wet dripping mouth, there was still hope. There were, Carly told herself, several reasons to hope.

The first was the cauterization that Dan Kelly had done. If it was done soon enough the burning could kill the terrible poison before it could begin to spread through the body.

The second reason to hope was a secret. Woo Ying had told her the secret, even though Aunt M. had told him not to. The secret was that Aunt M. was trying to find a regular doctor who would give Tiger the shots that had been developed by the French scientist Louis Pasteur. Aunt M. had tried a doctor in Ventura and had been turned down, but she had not given up and was waiting to hear from another in Los Angeles. It would be very expensive, but Woo Ying said that Aunt M. would find some way to pay for the treatment if she could find a doctor who would take a little dog as a patient. But Aunt M. didn't want Carly to get her hopes up before it was certain, so she had made Woo Ying promise not to tell. But he had forgotten his promise when he found Carly crying in the garden one day, and he'd told her all about it. And then he begged her not to tell that he'd broken his promise, because if she told Aunt M., the yelling wouldn't stop for a whole year. "Maybe two year," he said. "Aunty yell at Woo Ying for two year if you tell." So Carly had promised she wouldn't.

The last reason to hope was, perhaps, not a very good one. At least no one else seemed to think it was. But Carly thought there might be some reason to hope that the coyote had not had hydrophobia after all. The thing was, they had never found him. Even though the sheriff and his deputies had searched and searched, they had never found the coyote either living or dead. So there was just a slight chance, Carly reasoned, that he'd had some other disease that made him braver and meaner than coyotes usually were, and after he'd bitten Tiger he'd gone off into the hills somewhere and gotten well.

So the weeks crept by. Weeks of going to school and living at Greenwood but spending every spare minute at the ranch visiting Tiger and watching him—watching and worrying and counting the dangerous days. The wound on Tiger's leg from the cauterization, so much bigger and more noticeable than the bite had been, healed over and the white hair grew down around it until it could hardly be seen. Six weeks went by and then eight and it was Christmastime and Tiger was still living in his pen and looking and acting just the same as he always had.

Christmas was strange and sad that year. At Greenwood Aunt M. had the biggest tree ever, and she and Woo Ying made as big a fuss as usual about presents and Christmas cookies and all kinds of special things to eat. There was a tree at the ranch house, too, but it wasn't the same as other years, with Tiger still in danger and locked in his prison, and Mama still not well enough to come downstairs for Christmas dinner.

Carly, with Aunt M.'s help, had made Mama a beautiful new bed jacket covered with lacy ruffles. But when everyone went up to her room to watch her open her presents, she was tired from all the excitement and hardly looked at the jacket when Carly unwrapped it for her.

Then January came, and even though it was a long time yet before the six months were up, Carly couldn't help feeling more hopeful. He was such a little dog. Surely the poison, if it was there, would have reached his brain by now and the disease would have begun. As the cool, clear days of January crept by and Tiger went on being his funny, bouncy, begging, accusing, and forgiving self, Carly began to feel more and more hopeful that he was going to be all right.

But one Sunday morning in mid-January something was

183

different. When Carly came out for a short visit before breakfast, Tiger was lying, as he often did, in the corner of his pen.
But when she called to him he stayed where he was and she
noticed then that he was licking the side of an old chicken-
feed pan. He licked and licked at the pan and then he licked
his own feet and then the pan again and Carly had to call him
several times before he got up and came to the gate.

She didn't mention the difference to the rest of the family.
It probably didn't mean anything, and she didn't want them
to think it did. When she came back again briefly just before
leaving for church, he had stopped licking and was pacing up
and down at the far side of the pen. He stopped when she
talked to him and came to the gate, but as she walked away
she looked back and saw him pacing again, his head and tail
low and his funny eyebrows doing their sad, worried wiggle.

In church that day and again in her bed at Greenwood that
night she prayed longer and harder than she had ever prayed
before. She couldn't sleep and after a while she didn't even
try anymore, because every time she closed her eyes she
could see Tiger's pleading, worried eyes. At last she got up
and went to sit on the window seat, wrapped in her old
bunny-rabbit quilt.

It was a clear, cold night with a tiny crescent moon and
millions of stars, and then, while she watched, a star fell,
arching across the sky like a fiery arrow. Like an arrow—or
perhaps like an omen, or even a promise. Perhaps a promise
from God that Tiger would be all right. Soon afterward she
felt herself relaxing and slipping toward sleep, and she went
back to bed and slept until sunrise.

But the next morning when Lila arrived at Greenwood she
was in the surrey instead of the cart, and Father was with her.
Carly was waiting on the veranda and she stayed where she
was as he came up the path, with an aching rage beginning to

roar up out of some terrible depths, drowning her heart and mind.

Tiger was dead. Father had shot him. She heard that much before she ran away shrieking with pain and anger. They tried to stop her, Aunt M. and then Woo Ying, but she pushed them aside and went on running, up the stairs and down the hall to her room. She threw herself down on the bed and the strange sounds that were coming up out of her throat went on and on, deafening, strangling sounds that rasped her throat and throbbed in every part of her body.

Some time later Aunt M. was sitting on the edge of the bed, not touching or speaking but just sitting there quietly, and the howling pain had shriveled to a wavering moan that came and went as thought returned and with it all the sad and terrible questions. How had they known it was hydrophobia? Could they really have been sure so soon? Why had they done it without telling her? What if it they had been wrong and it had only been another sulking spell or the beginnings of some curable sickness like distemper? And then back to all the other old and hopeless what-ifs. What might have happened if she'd only thought of going for Dan Kelly sooner? And what if she hadn't stopped to talk to Henry that day by the cemetery? What if, what if, what if?

No one tried to make her go to school that day, and by noon she had stopped crying. She didn't want to come down to lunch—not because she wasn't hungry; to her surprise, she was—but she had finally managed to stop howling and she didn't want to begin again. It was as if the dark wound that had opened and released the shrieking pain had begun to heal over, but any kind of touching, even the most loving and sympathetic—especially the most loving and sympathetic—would tear it open again. But later when Woo Ying was in the garden and Aunt M. was napping, she crept down to the kitchen and ate ravenously.

Late that night when she had gone to bed, Aunt M. came in again and, without being asked, answered some of the terrible questions. She told first how Father had gone for Doc Booker and had insisted that he come out to the ranch, and how they had waited until there was no doubt. Until any more waiting would only have meant more terrible suffering. She talked, too, about her own secret plan and how it had failed. How she had tried to find a doctor who would give Tiger the Pasteur treatment, but how the Ventura doctor had refused and the Los Angeles man, who might have done it, was away on a trip to the East Coast and had not yet returned. Carly listened without speaking, and at last Aunt M. went away.

On Tuesday she went back to school, and all the business of daily life began again, and as the week went by the pain and grief receded until it was no longer an all-engulfing wave. It would always be there, she knew, a part of her that she would never be without, and which would always be painful to touch, but only a part now instead of the consuming anguish that had drowned her mind and heart.

On Wednesday after dinner Aunt M. began to talk about Trixie's puppies. Trixie had been a litter mate of Tiger's, the only one of the litter that the Bufords had kept. And now Trixie had four little pups of her own. Of course, they were just newborn and too young to leave their mother, but Aunt M. wanted to know if Carly would like to go out and look at them and see if—

But then Carly interrupted and said, "No. No I can't. Not —yet."

And Aunt M. said, "Of course, dear. I understand."

But that night in bed Carly found herself thinking about the Bufords' new puppies and wondering what they would look like and if any of them would ever be as smart as Tiger. She went on thinking about them off and on for the rest of the week, and on that very Friday morning she thought about them again when she happened to see Clarence Buford driving his father's team down Arnold Street.

It was on that same Friday morning that Mama died.

❈❈❈ *chapter 33*

They went out to the ranch in Aunt M.'s surrey. It was gray and drizzly, and Woo Ying was wearing a slicker. Carly and Aunt M. sat in back under the canopy with the side curtains down. Aunt M. was wearing a black dress that had been up in the attic since Uncle Edward died, but Carly was still dressed in the blue gingham she'd worn to school that day, with a wide black ribbon tied around her arm.

Almost all the way out to the ranch Aunt M. held both of Carly's hands in hers and talked about Mama. Carly sat very still and tried to think only about what Aunt M. was saying and nothing more. Aunt M. spoke about how Dr. Dodge had told the family in August that Mama didn't have long to live. It was heart failure, Aunt M. said. Congestive heart failure and not the weak lungs that Mama had always talked and worried about.

"I didn't know," Carly said. "No one told me. I thought it was only . . . the same as before."

"That was what they wanted you to think. They didn't want you to know she was dying. That was why Nellie asked

188

if you could stay at Greenwood. She didn't want you to know, and she felt she couldn't keep it from you if you were there all the time."

Carly nodded. She understood that now. She understood how Nellie had thought that knowing that Mama was dying would have been too much for her to bear. Of course, that was what Nellie would have thought. Carly turned her face away and closed her eyes. She knew Aunt M. was watching her. Even with her eyes closed she could see Aunt M.'s face. Clenching her fists and gritting her teeth, she tried to shut herself away from the pity and worry in Aunt M.'s eyes.

They were almost to the ranch when they met the hearse. Mr. Strickland, the undertaker, was driving the black horses, and as he drew near he raised his stovepipe hat and solemnly bowed his head. Aunt M. reached out for Carly. She let herself be pulled close so that her face was hidden, but not before she had seen it clearly.

She had seen the hearse before in funeral processions in Santa Luisa and on its way to the cemetery. So even with her eyes closed and her face smothered against Aunt M.'s bosom, she could see the shiny black van with its gleaming brass fittings and glass walls through which a flower-strewn coffin could be seen, except when black velvet curtains were drawn across the glass, as they were now. She had always cried when she saw it. It had been easy to cry then, thinking about death and grief and the poor dead person, whom she usually had known at least a little. But now, when it was Mama who lay behind the black curtains, she buried her face in Aunt M.'s cape and would not allow herself that kind of tears.

The ranch house was full of people. In the parlor with Father and Charles were Reverend Mapes and Mrs. Mapes and Mrs. Hamilton and all three of the Bufords. Everyone hugged Carly and kissed her, and some of them were crying.

Father was wearing his Sunday suit, but somehow it didn't

look the same, and neither did he. The suit that had always seemed so grand looked worn and wrinkled now, and Father's eyes, his fierce gray Hartwick eyes, were dull and uncertain. He seemed almost like a stranger, and when he took Carly's shoulders in both his hands and looked down at her, she suddenly felt frightened. He said her name, and something else, but her heart was pounding so hard that it echoed in her ears and blotted out the words. As soon as she could, she pulled away and went looking for Nellie.

In the kitchen Mrs. Purdy and Maggie Kelly were comforting Lila and Arthur, and no one noticed Carly, so she ducked back into the hall and went upstairs to Nellie's room.

Nellie was sitting on the edge of her bed, crouched over and shriveled down like an animal in pain. Her face was red and wet and her eyes were blank and swollen. She wasn't making any sound, but Carly could almost hear the terrible noise that throbbed in her throat, fighting to get out. Hearing that silent sound made Carly begin to cry.

She cried for a long time, and Nellie put her arms around her and rocked her to and fro. The tears, Carly's tears, were real and painful, and it wasn't until later that night, back home at Greenwood, that she realized that they really hadn't made any difference—and why.

The funeral was on Sunday afternoon, and after the ceremony at the church everyone went out to the cemetery. It was a warm day for February, and under the oak and eucalyptus trees the earth was rain-softened and carpeted with fresh new grass. The mourners left their surreys and buggies in the long avenue that led to the central knoll, and went on foot to the Carlton plot. Inside the plot the grass had been mowed to a smooth lawn, and the mourners in their black suits and dresses formed a dark, silent circle around the open grave.

The pallbearers came then, Father and Charles and Arthur, and Dan Kelly and Mr. Buford and Clarence, and lowered

190

the coffin down into the earth between Uncle Edward's granite monument and Petey's tombstone. There was no wind in the trees, and after Reverend Mapes stopped speaking, it was very quiet except for the soft murmur of the creek and now and then the sound of crying.

Nearly everyone was crying, and Carly could have too. Standing by the grave, dressed in the lumpy black dress with its high stiff collar that Father had picked out for her at the Emporium, it would have been easy to be the poor orphaned child, weeping over her mother's tomb. It would have been easy to water the grave with bitter tears, as she had done so many times for Petey. But she didn't let herself do it.

Then everyone went home and Carly went back to Greenwood with Aunt M. and Woo Ying and life began again, almost the same as before. But not really the same. At least not for Carly.

On Tuesday she went back to school, wearing the black mourning dress, and on that first day Mr. Alderson and Miss Pruitt and all the students came one by one to tell her how sorry they were. While they were talking she held her face very still and stiff, and when they had finished she nodded and said "Thank you" and nothing more. For several days after that everyone was solemn and quiet when she was around, even Emma Hawkins and Henry Quigley Babcock.

She wore the black dress all that week, but on Friday when she got home from school Aunt M. came into the kitchen carrying a new dress. She held it up to Carly to see if it would fit. It was a beautiful dress with tiny pale green stripes, a braid-trimmed bolero, and big puffed sleeves.

"Yes!" Aunt M. said. "I thought so. Suits you perfectly. Now go upstairs and try it on. And when you get out of the dreadful black thing, give it to Woo Ying to make mop rags."

"But Father said—"

"Never mind that. Tell him I put my foot down. Foolish

custom, mourning. Going around reminding yourself and everyone else to grieve. Particularly where children are concerned. Wear your ordinary dresses, child, and smile again. We miss that smile of yours, don't we, Woo Ying?"

So Carly stopped wearing black, and when Father saw her he hardly seemed to notice. And at school it wasn't long before everyone began to treat her just as they had before— except for Henry Babcock, who was behaving strangely.

It wasn't that Henry had really reformed, because he was still tormenting everyone else as much as ever. But he didn't pull Carly's hair anymore, or push things off her desk, and he'd stopped calling her Mehitabel in his normally nasty tone of voice. Carly knew there was something unnatural about Henry's behavior but she didn't know what was behind it, so she simply went on ignoring him as she always had.

Sometimes Matt, on his way home on Rosemary, stopped to talk to Carly as she waited for Lila. Usually he talked about school things or about what had been happening at Grizzly Flats. But once he said his grandpa had been up in the Sespe again and had seen five condors in flight at one time.

"I was thinking," Matt said, "that if we went up to the spring pretty soon we might—"

"No!" Carly interrupted. She hadn't meant to say it so fiercely, but the thought of condors brought back that bright fall day when she had been so sure she would see them dancing. Looking at Matt's startled face she said "No" in a more ordinary manner. Matt nodded, looking puzzled, and didn't mention condors again for a long time.

On Saturdays Carly still went to the ranch on Chloe and helped Nellie and Lila with housework and sewing. Sometimes she swept and dusted and sometimes she helped with the baking, and when Duchess had her new little heifer calf, she was the one who taught it to drink from a pail. Clarence Buford had started coming to the ranch every Saturday evening to sit in the parlor and talk to Father and Nellie, and sometimes just to Nellie alone. Lila had begun work on a beautiful white dress that was covered with tucks and ruffles and panels of lace, and sometimes Carly helped with the pinning and basting. Lila was still wearing black, but she said the dress was for high school graduation in June, and Father had agreed that she could be out of mourning by then.

The days went by and everything was the same and yet not the same, and the changes began to seem more and more normal. Some of the differences were definite improvements if looked at from certain points of view—improvements like industry and diligence and self-control. Carly was working harder at school as well as at home, and spending less time chattering and playing and daydreaming. Particularly less time daydreaming.

It wasn't that she enjoyed scrubbing and ironing and dividing fractions any more than she had before, or even that working hard made her feel any better. It was just that work felt safer now, and dreams more risky.

❧❀❧ *chapter 34*

It was on a Friday early in March that Alfred Quigley came to Greenwood to talk to Aunt M. He came in the Quigleys' fancy phaeton, and after he'd tied the grays to the hitching post, he and Henry Quigley Babcock came to the front door. Carly had seen them from the window, and she decided to go to her room and stay there. But in just a few minutes Woo Ying knocked and said that Aunt M. wanted her in the parlor. And there they were—Alfred and Henry.

It was a cold day, and Alfred Quigley was wearing a Prince Albert coat and a wide silk tie, and Henry was still in his school shoes and knickers instead of his after-school overalls. As soon as Carly came into the room, Henry looked at his grandfather and then stood up and began to talk, as if he were reciting at an entertainment.

Afterward Carly couldn't remember all of what Henry said, because she had known immediately what it was going to be about and she didn't want to hear it. So she stood perfectly still in the doorway, and all the time Henry was talking she was silently saying *Stop! Stop! I don't want to hear you* over and over again. And even though she didn't say the words out loud, they echoed so loudly inside her head that she missed some of what Henry was saying about how sorry he was about Tiger, and also how sorry he was about the float and the firecrackers, and how he had asked God to forgive him and God had, and he hoped Carly did too.

When he finally stopped talking, Carly nodded and turned to Aunt M. and asked, "May I go now?"

She hadn't meant to be rude, but she was so desperate to get away that she didn't realize what was expected of her until Aunt M. said, "Of course, child. But you do forgive Henry, don't you?"

So she said quickly, "Yes. I do. I forgive him. I forgive you, Henry," and then she turned and ran upstairs and back to her room. She was still lying on her bed thinking about God's forgiveness and whether it was useless to ask for it if you didn't deserve it, when Aunt M. called her to come to dinner.

In the kitchen the table was set with the best china and silver, just as it had been when Woo Ying had made a celebration because Carly was coming back to live at Greenwood. As soon as she came into the room, Carly could see how excited Aunt M. and Woo Ying were and they both began to talk at once, telling her about what had happened. It seemed that one of the reasons Alfred Quigley had come was to say that he had removed his objections and Aunt M. was now a member of the water company.

She knew how important it was. She knew perfectly well that it meant that now Father could plant citrus on the Carlton lowland, and water the apricots and walnuts in dry years, and that the hard times would soon be over for the Hartwicks and Aunt M. too. It meant that the ranch house could have a new indoor toilet and all the other things it needed. And Arthur could go to college and Lila could also, if she wanted to, which she probably didn't unless Johnny was going too. Listening to Aunt M. and Woo Ying, Carly kept reminding herself that she should be as excited as they were and as happy too.

Later Aunt M. and Woo Ying began to talk about the funny things both of the Quigleys had said. They laughed about the way Henry had announced that God had forgiven him, as if his grandpa had sent God a telegram and got back an answer by return mail. And Woo Ying stood up and stuck out his chest and imitated the grand and lordly way Alfred Quigley had made his announcement about the water company. And Carly laughed as much and as hard as they did, or least she tried to, and for a while she thought she'd succeeded. But after Carly was in bed that night, Aunt M. came into her room, pulled a chair up beside the bed, and sat down.

"Carly, child," she said, "I'm worried about you. And Woo Ying is too. I wonder—"

"I'm fine," Carly interrupted. "I'm just the same as always."

Aunt M. shook her head. "No. You're not. You're not my high-stepping little colt anymore."

Carly giggled. "I'm not a colt. I'm a filly. And look. I can step as high as ever. Just watch." And she jumped out of bed and pranced around the room in her nightgown, lifting her knees high and tossing her head.

Aunt M. laughed, and when Carly stopped prancing, she tucked her back in bed and kissed her forehead. Then she straightened up with her hand on her back, as she always did, and said, "About those puppies, Carly. They must be just about old enough to leave their mother now, and—"

"No!" Carly shouted. Burying her face in the pillow, she pounded her fists on the bed and tried to smother the sound of her own voice saying "No, no, no" over and over again.

Then Aunt M. was sitting beside her and trying to lift her up, but she kept her head down and her arms up around her face, hiding it from sight.

"What is it, child? Tell me. Please tell me," Aunt M. said.

She wanted to tell. She wanted to so badly and for a moment she thought she would, but it was too awful, and when she finally rolled over and let Aunt M. brush the hair out of her face and wipe away the tears, she only shook her head and said, "I can't."

❧❀❧ *chapter 35*

Being a member of the water company began to change
things at Greenwood, as well as at the ranch, almost immediately. Even when the pipes that would carry water to the
Carlton land were still going in, the changes had already begun. Because there would now be water for her land, Aunt
M. could get a loan at the bank, and out at the ranch two or
three new hired men were soon at work getting the land
ready for the first lemon trees. Arthur was still working at the
Emporium but he was beginning to write letters to colleges,
and Woo Ying was talking constantly about the new motorcar
Aunt M. was going to buy before very long.

There were other changes, too, now that Father and Aunt
M. were going to the water-company meetings and talking
with the Quigley-Babcocks in person instead of through lawyers in the courthouse. Aunt M. said that they'd ironed out
some old misunderstandings and that at the meetings Father
and Alfred Quigley sometimes actually found themselves on
the same side of an argument.

"Always seems to surprise them," Aunt M. said. "Not to

mention everyone else. Disappoints a few people, too, I daresay. What are the gossips going to have to keep their tongues busy, with the Carlton-Quigley feud fizzling out like this?"

Late that March it began to look as if another important change was about to happen when there began to be rumors that telephone lines were about to go up in the Hamilton Valley.

"I must say," Aunt M. said, "when Alfred Bennington Quigley has a change of heart he doesn't do it halfway. I hear now that he's decided to let them run the telephone lines across his valley land. What do you think of that?"

Carly said she thought it was wonderful, and Woo Ying said something in Chinese that didn't sound nearly as rude as the things he usually said when Alfred Quigley was mentioned. And just a day or two later when Carly came home from school Aunt M. told her to dial 216.

"That's the new number," she said, "out at the ranch. Nellie rang me an hour or so ago. Said she wanted to talk to you when you got home."

So Carly cranked the phone and told Bessie Taylor, the operator, that she wanted 216, and in a minute she heard Nellie saying hello.

"Isn't it exciting," Nellie said, and Carly agreed with her, and after they'd talked for a minute or two Nellie said she was just leaving to come into town and could she stop by for a visit. So Carly asked and Aunt M. looked up from the beans she was snapping and said, "Yes, of course," and for some reason Carly suddenly felt certain that Aunt M. had already known that Nellie was coming and she also knew why. Carly found out why soon after Nellie arrived.

When Nellie came down the path, Aunt M. was out in the garden bothering Woo Ying while he planted the spring flowers, and she only waved to Nellie and told her to go on in. And as soon as Nellie had hugged and kissed Carly, she led her into the parlor and sat down beside her on the love seat.

"Carly," she said, reaching out to hold Carly's hands, "we're all worried about you. Aunt M., Woo Ying, myself, Father—everyone is very concerned."

"About me? Why?" Carly said.

"Because you're just not our Carly anymore." Nellie's blue eyes were smiling, but it was easy to see the worried pain behind the smile. Nellie had had enough pain. Carly wasn't going to add to it by telling her the awful, unbearable truth.

"I am," she said, trying to return Nellie's smile. "I'm fine, really I am."

Nellie shook her head. "I know how hard these last few months have been for you. For all of us. But you're so young and you've always had so much—so much—life and joy and —Hartwick spirit, as Aunt M. calls it. And now it's all dimmed and pale. What is it?"

"No," Carly said stubbornly. "It's nothing."

And then Nellie got mad. "Carly Hartwick! If you're just feeling sorry for yourself—making up games about your great tragedies—when we've all, the whole family has been through so much—I'm going to—I'm just going to . . ." She reached out and took Carly by the shoulders and shook her, and Carly opened her mouth and wailed and let the secret be shaken out in a great howling rush.

"I didn't cry," she wailed. "I didn't cry when Mama died."

Nellie's anger was gone in a second. "Oh, baby. Of course you did. We cried and cried together. In my room. Remember?"

"No. No. That was later. And that was for you. I was crying for you because I saw how you felt. But I didn't cry before, when they first told me about Mama."

Nellie put her arms around Carly and rocked her the way

200

she'd done that day in her room. "People don't always cry when someone dear to them dies. Sometimes there is grief too great for tears. Or sometimes they can only cry much later. Sometimes people feel too much to cry."

Carly shook her head. "No. Not too much. I felt something—sad—sad for Mama—and for you—and Father, and for myself, too, I guess, but it wasn't like . . ." She couldn't bear to go on.

"Like you felt when Tiger died?"

Carly hung her head. "I howled," she said. "Or something howled. It was as if I wasn't there anymore. Nothing was there except the . . . pain and that terrible noise."

"I know," Nellie said, "I know, baby."

She raised her head then and looked straight at Nellie and said, "And when my own mother died I didn't even cry."

Nellie returned her stare for a moment and then shut her eyes and bit her lip and rocked herself to and fro. Suddenly she jumped up and began to walk around the room. For a long time she walked back and forth, shaking her head and frowning, and then she came back and sat beside Carly again. She looked angry.

"No," she said. "Not your own mother. Anna Hartwick was not your mother, Carly. Oh, I don't mean she didn't give birth to you, because she did, but your mother was Aunt M. And Woo Ying. Woo Ying is much much more your mother than Mama ever was."

"Woo Ying?" Carly couldn't help smiling at the thought of Woo Ying's being anybody's mother.

"Yes. It was Aunt M. and Woo Ying who gave you the kind of love and care that babies need."

"But I loved Mama. I really did."

"Of course you did. But not as if she'd really been a mother to you."

Carly nodded. She looked at Nellie's bright blue eyes and

remembered how they had looked on the day Mama died. "But she was a mother to you, and to Charles and Arthur and Lila?" She didn't mean it to be a question, but it almost was.

"Yes. When we were little. Mama was good with little babies, I think. At least until Petey died. And then—well, after that I guess things became reversed. After that it was as if I were the mother and she became my child."

"Oh, Nellie," Carly said. She was thinking that when Mama died Nellie had lost both her mother and her child. Carly threw her arms around her sister and began to cry.

Carly and Nellie were still sitting on the love seat and crying, with their arms around each other, when a voice said, "Well, if this isn't a dreary scene. If you two young ladies intend to keep this up, you can just come on out in the kitchen where the furniture is waterproof." Aunt M. had her hands on her hips and she was frowning.

Nellie jumped up and said, "Aunt M. I—" But before she got any farther Aunt M. had marched out of the room.

"Oh, dear," Nellie said. "I'm afraid she's dreadfully angry. She asked me to come down and try to cheer you up. And it must have looked like all I did was upset you even more. I'd best go talk to her."

Wiping her eyes and gulping, Carly said, "No. I'll talk to her. It'll be all right. You know how Aunt M. is."

"Yes, I guess I do know," Nellie said. "And I'm sure you can make her understand. So I guess I'll be getting on into town before the Emporium closes."

She got out her handkerchief and wiped her eyes and then kissed Carly and hugged her and hurried toward the front door. But in the hall she stopped suddenly and came back.

"I haven't just upset you more, have I?" Nellie's freckled forehead was crinkled with worry. "Telling someone that their mother never really loved them is a terrible way to try to cheer them up. Sometimes I think I always say and do the wrong thing."

"Nellie Hartwick!" Carly said. "You stop that this minute. Stop being such a worry-wart. You did too cheer me up. I promise you did."

And it was true too. Standing by the window and watching Nellie as she hurried down the garden path, Carly felt sure something was better, and she also felt sure she would understand just what it was as soon as she'd had time to think about it.

At the gate Nellie turned and looked back toward the house, and as she stood there with one hand on the gate and with the bright sunshine making a gleaming halo of her flyaway red hair, she suddenly looked so beautiful that Carly caught her breath in surprise. She'd never thought of Nellie as beautiful before. Lila, yes, but not Nellie. But now suddenly it seemed to Carly that Nellie's bright stormy beauty was much more exciting than Lila's, even if Nellie would never look like a pale polished cameo in the moonlight.

In the kitchen Aunt M. was making tea, still frowning. "What in God's name was going on in there? What did Nellie say to upset you like that?"

"It wasn't what she said that made me cry," Carly said. And then she began to tell Aunt M. all about the conversation with Nellie. Her own confession was easier the second time, and she didn't hang her head as she told Aunt M. about how she'd hated herself for her terrible heartlessness.

All the time Carly was talking, Aunt M. stood perfectly still with the teapot in her hand while the kettle boiled and steamed away on the range. But when it was all told she made a harrumphing sound and nodded her head sharply.

"Heartlessness! Now that's the silliest thing I ever heard of. There never has been a child with a heart any bigger than yours, Carly Hartwick, and there never will be. Now, what I call heartless is a woman who would hold her own grief and disappointment against a helpless baby. She never wanted you, Carly. She didn't want to get over Petey's death. And when your father and Doctor Dodge, too, told her that a new baby would cure her grief she just set herself to prove them wrong. And . . . well, there, I've said enough. Too much, probably," and Aunt M. clamped her lips together and went to get the kettle off the stove.

She kept her lips clamped like that while she poured the tea water and got out some sugar biscuits, but as she sat down at the table she sighed deeply and said, "Poor child! Poor overburdened, put-upon child!"

"Overburdened," Carly said, eagerly. "That's what's been wrong with me. I've been feeling—"

"I didn't mean you, you silly goose," Aunt M. said. "You're not in the least overburdened, and never have been. And if you're planning to start being dramatic about how your mother never loved you, you can just stop it right now, because plenty of other people loved you from the very start. I was talking about your poor sister. Well, well. I've a notion that Nellie's talk with you may do her as much good as it did you. Seems to me she faced up to some things she should have seen for what they were years ago."

Carly sat down at the kitchen table and began to poke some biscuit crumbs around with one finger. Being called a silly goose when she'd just made such a difficult confession didn't seem fair. Looking up at Aunt M. from under angry eyebrows, she decided to get even.

"Nellie said that Woo Ying is my mother most of all. More than anybody else—my mother is Woo Ying."

"And so he is," Aunt M. said. "Would you like a cup of tea, dear, or do you just plan to sit there and pout?"

❧❋❧ *chapter 36*

What Nellie had said about Mama was on Carly's mind all the rest of that day and now and then on the next, even during school. On two different occasions she had to ask Mr. Alderson to repeat a question because she hadn't been listening. After the second time he made some pointed comments about springtime "daydreamers," and during recess Mavis said that Carly was acting awfully peculiar, almost as if she were in love, or something.

She was still trying to sort it out when Matt asked again if she wanted to go looking for condors. It was on the Friday before the spring holidays and she was waiting for Lila in front of the school, just as she'd been the last time he'd asked, and actually she started the conversation herself. But only because she had something for Rosemary.

"Matt," she called, "wait a minute."

Matt pulled up so quickly that Rosemary bunched her neat little hooves and skidded on the gravelly road. "What d'you want?" Matt said.

Carly was fishing around in her lunch pail. "I have something for Rosemary. I saved her my apple core."

While Rosemary munched the apple core, Carly noticed that Matt was frowning at her in a thoughtful way as if he were trying to decide something. And sure enough, a moment later he said, "I—I don't suppose you'd be wanting to look for condors again? During spring vacation, I mean?"

Carly was surprised. Matt hadn't said much of anything to her since she'd turned him down so fiercely the last time he'd asked if she wanted to go exploring. Afterward she'd been sorry about yelling at him, but she hadn't wanted to explain why she'd done it, or even known how to, so she didn't say anything at all.

But she didn't want to hurt his feelings again, even though the thought of starting out on another exploring trip brought back memories—memories of the day when she and Tiger started out together and she'd been so sure they were going to see the condors. So all she said was "I don't know. I'll be at Greenwood most of the time. I'd have to ask Aunt M."

Matt looked pleased. Carly didn't mention that Aunt M. would almost certainly say no.

But Aunt M. said yes. Carly was amazed. "He wants to go up to the spring," she said. "Carlton Spring. It's quite a long way."

"Condor Spring," Aunt M. said. "And I know how far it is. Edward and I rode up there many times."

"I didn't know you called it Condor Spring."

Aunt M. smiled. "All us old-timers call it that," she said. "Yes, I think you should go. Just be sure to tell Dan Kelly what trail you'll be taking and how long you'll be gone."

So Carly and Matt left Grizzly Flats at midmorning of a warm spring day on their way to Condor Spring. Carly had ridden Chloe as far as the Kelly ranch and stopped in for a while for a visit with Dan and Maggie. While Matt unsaddled

Chloe and put her in the barn, and got the donkeys ready to go, Carly drank milk and ate gingerbread in Maggie's kitchen and listened to Dan tell about his last trip into the mountains. It was cozy and comfortable in the kitchen, and Carly found herself in no hurry to leave. Matt was fretting, saying they'd not have any chance at all to see the condors dancing if they didn't get going, but Carly stayed where she was—until Dan took Matt's side.

"Well, then, off with ye," Dan said, pushing back his chair and going to the door. "Time's a-flying and 'tis a longish way you have to go."

Dan, too, Carly thought. It seemed odd that first Aunt M. and now the Kellys should be so determined to make her go to the spring. Not that she didn't want to. It was just . . . With the thought still unfinished Carly let Dan boost her up on Rosemary—Matt had insisted that she should ride Rosemary, although, strictly speaking, it wasn't her turn—and they were off.

It was a beautiful day. The world was green with spring except where lupines and California poppies turned whole hillsides purple and orange. In the shady depths of the canyons large ferns lifted their graceful fronds beside rainwater streams that still trickled down to the valley below.

But Carly's mood didn't match the day. She was trying hard to act normal, and when Matt pointed out things like the wildflowers or raccoon tracks or jackrabbits, she made an effort to be interested, but he seemed to know there was something wrong. He asked her once if she was mad at him and she said, "No, silly. Why should I be mad at you?"

It was the truth too. She wasn't angry, or sad, or even scared, really. It was just that she found it hard to believe that anything good was going to happen.

The sun was almost directly overhead when the donkeys slid down the last incline to where, under the sheltering shade of oaks and cottonwoods, the clear spring water filled the shallow pool. But nothing stirred and there was no sound except for the trickle of water and the faint whisper of the breeze among the branches.

"Nothing there yet," Matt said. "Come on." He kicked Barney in the ribs and the old donkey headed for the pool at a trot.

The NO TRESPASSING sign was still there, its message blurred by knife scratches, and nothing remained of the dead condor. But at one edge of the pool the damp earth was crisscrossed by blurred indentations, and floating near the bank was an enormous black feather.

"See," Matt said excitedly. "They've been here. Not long ago, I betcha."

Carly nodded. "I know," she said, and for a moment hope flared. Maybe, just maybe, something wonderful would happen after all.

While Matt led the donkeys downstream to a little meadow and hobbled them, Carly picked out a good lookout spot behind a tall stand of ferns, and when Matt returned they settled down to watch and wait. They ate their picnic lunch and watched some more, and then they played mumblety-peg with Matt's pocket knife. After that they caught frogs and raced them by putting them in the middle of a circle to see whose frog would be first to reach the edge. When the frogs escaped, they built bark boats and floated them on the pool.

Even without condors it should have been a good day. And it was, too, except that . . . except that the strange, uneasy feeling was still there, like a dark cloud that would never quite go away. And no condors swooped in to land beside the pool with a great rush of wind and whisper of gigantic feathers. At last, when the sun had begun to sink behind the high ridge to the west, Matt said, "Well, I reckon they're not going to come," and Carly agreed with him, thinking to herself that she'd never really believed that they would. But all she said was "I guess not. Let's go get the donkeys."

The donkeys had moved downstream following the deeper grass that grew beside the water, and when Matt and Carly found them they were grazing happily in the deep shade of the valley floor. Matt was down on his knees removing Rosemary's hobbles when, for no particular reason, Carly glanced up at the sky—and there they were.

Just above the deeply shadowed canyon three huge birds seemed to be floating eastward on shafts of sunlight. "Look! Look, Matt!" Carly gasped and sank down into the tall grass. Still on his knees, Matt tipped his head backward and his mouth fell open. "Lordy." He gasped. "Condors."

The air was clear and reddish-gold and the condors seemed, not near, but magnified by the brilliant light. Flying in against the sun, the huge black birds were haloed with sunset. Triangles of white beneath their wings gleamed like snow, and long fringes of finger feathers tilted from shiny black to mirrored gold. Sweeping down over the spot where Carly lay in the deep shadow, the first condor tipped into a sweeping turn, soared over the second bird, under the third, and turned to pass them again and again. For an immeasurable length of time the three condors rode the air currents with effortless grace, soaring and turning and soaring again in an intricate pattern of movement like winged dancers in an airborne minuet.

When the gigantic birds finally drifted westward and disappeared over the crest of the hills, Carly stayed where she was, staring up into the sunlit distance. She didn't want it to end—the beauty and high excitement and the brief escape into a far bright freedom. Slowly and reluctantly she came back to the coolness of the grass, the munching of the grazing donkeys, and the shadows of the valley floor.

"Carly"—Matt's voice was questioning, worried—"we'd best be going. It's getting late. Are you all right?"

Carly sat up, smiling. "Yes," she said. "I'm all right. Let's go."

They didn't talk much on the way home, and what they did say was about other things, ordinary things like the history test that Mr. Alderson had scheduled for right after the end of vacation. But when they were back at Grizzly Flats and Carly was up on Chloe, getting ready to leave, Matt said, "Well, it was a good day?" and made it into a question.

Carly nodded. "A good day," she said with certainty.

"Even if we didn't see them dancing?"

"Next time," she said. "Next time for sure."

"Well, maybe not for sure. You can't count on what condors will do."

Carly tugged on the reins and whirled Chloe into a trot. "Yes, I can, Matt Kelly," she called back over her shoulder. "I can count on condors if I want to."

❋❋❋ *chapter 37*

Carly didn't tell Aunt M. and Woo Ying about the condors that night at dinner, except to say that she'd seen them, and where, and what they'd been doing. The part she didn't try to tell was the way she'd felt about them and how important it had been. It wasn't that she didn't want to tell. It was just that she couldn't think of a way to put it into words.

That night in bed she decided to try again. Aunt M. had been in to say good night, and as she was going out the door Carly called her back. "Aunt M.," she said, "you know, I've been thinking . . ."

Aunt M. came back and stood by the foot of the bed with her hands on her hips. "And what have you been thinking, child?" she said.

"I've been thinking . . ." Carly said. She still couldn't find a way to explain about the condors. But there was something else. "It's about those puppies," she said.